Those
Miller
Girls!

Those Miller Girls!

BY ALBERTA WILSON CONSTANT

ILLUSTRATED BY JOE AND BETH KRUSH

THOMAS Y. CROWELL COMPANY • NEW YORK

BY THE AUTHOR

Miss Charity Comes to Stay
Willie and the Wildcat Well
Those Miller Girls!

This book is lovingly dedicated to the memory of my stepfather, Walter Clifton Erwin, who was born in Brown County, Kansas.

Chapter 1

Down the road came the Great Smith. A trail of dust whipped into the air behind it. Professor Cyrus Miller gripped the wheel and muttered, "Mind over matter. That's all there is to it. Mind over matter."

In the back seat his daughters, Lou Emma and Maddy, held tight to each other's hands.

"Faster," Maddy called, "faster, Papa."

"No," Lou Emma gulped, "not so fast, Papa."

But Lou Emma's words were lost forever in the wind that grabbed them from her mouth and scattered them down the road. Fifteen miles an hour. Twenty. On either side the world of Kansas streamed past. Little towns, tall fields of corn, green pastures, wheat stubble. A farmer pulled his wagon off the road

as the Great Smith roared past. In 1909 horses often
bolted at the sight of autos. Lou Emma felt embar-
rassed at the frightened team. Back in Auden, Ohio,
where they had lived all their lives, the Miller family
horse had reared and bucked when autos came near,
and she knew how the farmer felt.

But now everything was different. Today they
owned an auto . . . an auto manufactured in Topeka, Kansas, capital of the state where they were
going to live. To own an auto, to move to Gloriosa,
Kansas, where their father was going to teach history
at Eastern Kansas Classical College, and above all,
not to have any more housekeepers but to do everything themselves . . . all those things were so different that Lou Emma felt giddy listing them. Better to
think about one thing at a time. The Great Smith.

Yesterday when they got off the train in Topeka
they took a hack to the place where the Great Smith
was made. A salesman greeted them.

"Something small, inexpensive, and not showy,"
Professor Miller told him. "I'm a history teacher, not
a speed demon."

"Yes sir," the salesman agreed and started toward
the back of the building. Suddenly, Professor Miller
stopped, and the girls stopped, too. All three of them
stared at the wonderful machine.

It was a four-cylinder touring car finished in bril-

liant red. The top was folded back showing the quilted black leather cushions. Brass gleamed on the oil sidelights and the square nose of the engine. The gearshift lever was polished brass. A horn with a rubber bulb perched on the driver's side. Without a word Professor Miller walked over and squeezed the horn bulb.

"Oo-*oo*-gah . . . oo-*oo*-gah."

The deep-throated voice of the Great Smith gave Lou Emma goosebumps.

"Buy it, Papa, buy it. Buy it, Papa, buy it," Maddy murmured.

"Buy it, Papa, buy it," Lou Emma joined the soft-voiced chant.

"It's the first auto to climb Pike's Peak," the salesman said.

Professor Miller took out his bankbook, then slipped it back into his pocket. "There's no use asking if we can afford it. We can't. Let's put the question this way: Does the Miller family want this great, gaudy, monstrous machine?"

The girls hurled themselves on him and hugged him till he begged for mercy. "All right," he said. "As Julius Caesar might have put it, 'I came, I saw, I was conquered.' "

"A linen duster goes with it and a pair of goggles," the salesman said.

Professor Miller slipped his six-foot length into the cream-colored duster, and put on the goggles. At once he became a man of mystery.

"You look like the Arrow Collar man," Lou Emma admired him.

"You don't look a bit like a college professor," Maddy said.

"Thank you both," Professor Miller said. "I'm glad that I've never been a man to resist flattery. Crank 'er up and let's go before I regain my senses."

"Have you driven one of our machines before?" the salesman asked.

"I've never driven anything but a horse and buggy. But there's nothing to it, is there? You just push in the thingamajig, pull down the willipus-wallipus. Mind over matter, young man, mind over matter."

"There are a few things . . ."

In the end there were so many things that to get them straight took the whole day. While their father learned to drive, the Miller girls went out to see Topeka.

They circled the statehouse, looking at the high dome above it. They sat in the park and made up jokes about the passersby. They went to the Five and Ten. A Five and Ten in a new town is more exciting than one where every item is familiar. Each girl had a dollar, but the decision to break a round silver dollar into little bits of change was too hard to make. Anyway, the silver dollars were gifts from Aunt Jesse and she would never approve of anything they would buy in the Five and Ten.

Aunt Jesse had come down from Cleveland to tell them goodbye, and she had wept when she gave them the money and called them her poor little motherless nieces. Being called a poor little motherless anything is hard to endure; still, a dollar is a dollar, and the Miller girls had stood politely. Maddy had handed her aunt the cut-glass vial of smelling salts she always used when she got upset, and Lou Emma had found her white handkerchief.

"It took so long to get to the dollar, I thought she'd forgot," Maddy told their father.

"She told us three times how terrible living in

Kansas was going to be," Lou Emma said. "But I only listened once."

Professor Miller's lips had twitched but he hadn't laughed. He said what he always did, "Girls, Jesse means well."

At five o'clock in the morning they went to the Harvey House for breakfast before they started from Topeka to Gloriosa. Seventy-five miles was a long trip. The Great Smith's top speed was thirty miles an hour, but the salesman said they would not reach that often. The condition of the roads beyond Topeka was anybody's guess.

The long, lonesome whistle of the Santa Fe trains sounded in the Harvey House as they ate pancakes and bacon. Because it was a special day they were allowed to omit oatmeal. Maddy wondered where the trains were going.

"Going west," her father said. "Never forget that smart old geezer, what's-his-name, who said 'Go west, young man, and grow up with the country.' "

"Horace Greeley," Maddy supplied promptly. "Are you a young man, Papa?"

"It depends on when you ask me. I'm thirty-five. When I talk to old Dr. Moody at Auden I feel like a downy chick. But when I went back to Yale for my class reunion and looked at all those bright-eyed undergraduates I felt as old as Methuselah. No, older."

Lou Emma swabbed up her last drop of syrup with her last bite of pancake. She knew what her father meant, even if she was only twelve, and that wasn't near Methuselah's nine hundred sixty-nine. There were days when the bacon burned, when every pair of stockings developed a hole, when Maddy wouldn't play fair about taking turns, and their father's nose was so deep in a new book he didn't know anything was happening. But with all that she was glad they weren't going to have a house-keeper. And a little bit glad, too, even though she knew she shouldn't be, that they were going too far from Cleveland, Ohio, for Aunt Jesse to come to see them.

A little group of people had gathered outside the Harvey House to look at the Great Smith. They watched respectfully as Professor Miller stowed the girls in the back seat with their suitcases and arranged his books on the front seat. There were four text-books on history for him to look over—he was death on textbooks, the girls knew—and the big green *History of Greece* that the girls called H-O-G because of its size and the letters on the spine. A dozen apples, six for the front seat, six for the back. A boy in the group asked if he might crank the Great Smith, and slipped the hanging crank into place and gave it a mighty whirl. The engine responded with a growl, the people moved back on the sidewalk, and the Miller family was rolling down the wide streets of Topeka.

Soon stores and business buildings were behind them, and they were passing homes set far back on wide green lawns. An iron deer peeked from the shrubbery. The red and yellow spikes of cannas bloomed in flower beds. A little boy yelled, "Git a horse!"

"Remember when we used to do that?" Lou Emma said.

Maddy slid across the black leather seat. "Lou Emma, there's going to be a barrelful of people to meet in Gloriosa. I've got an idea about 'em."

"Hush. I don't want to hear about 'em," Lou Emma shuddered. Meeting new people was the hardest thing she had to do. "I don't want to meet any of 'em. Not even the Queen of Kansas."

"Kansas doesn't have a Queen, that I know of. Anyway, if you meet her all you have to do is speak up, and shake hands. Really shake hands, not like a dead fish."

"S'pose I feel like a dead fish? And s'pose I open my mouth and nothing comes out. Not . . . one . . . thing."

"That's why I've got this idea. We can fix up a

piece for you to memorize. The way we do in the Sunday School program."

Lou Emma sighed. "Couldn't I just say 'Dee-lighted'? When Teddy Roosevelt was president of the United States he said, 'Dee-lighted.' What's good enough for him is good enough for me—and the Queen of Kansas."

"No." Maddy wasn't satisfied. "You don't have the teeth he did. In pictures when he said 'Dee-lighted,' he kind of stuck his teeth out."

To Lou Emma's relief, Maddy let the subject drop. They were nearing the edge of the city. The houses were small and squatty, now, and the lawns patchy. The brick-paved street ended with a bump. And then came the dust.

The dust boiled up behind them and the wind whisked it around so that a fine gray coat of dust covered everything in the auto. Even the apples had a gritty taste to the peeling.

The grass grew near the edge of the road and from it grasshoppers whirred in. One of them hit Lou Emma in the neck. Maddy grabbed him and made him spit tobacco juice. Lou Emma tried it with the next grasshopper but she misjudged his spitting power and got a brown stain on her dress. Then grasshoppers lost their novelty as they whirred into the auto by the dozen.

"I've figured out what you can say when you meet people in Gloriosa," Maddy announced. She put a fixed smile on her face. " 'I'm Professor Miller's daughter and I'm very glad to be here.' Try it."

Lou Emma repeated mournfully, "I'm Professor Miller's daughter and I'm very glad to be here."

"That's awful. You've got to smile if it kills you. If you can't smile, laugh. Anybody can say 'ha-ha' same as they say in the funny papers."

"I'm Professor Miller's daughter . . . ha-ha . . .

and I'm very glad to be here," Lou Emma said.
"How's that?"

"It's all right if you can't do any better."

"I can't," Lou Emma said, "and I won't."

The Kansas wind, and the wind the auto stirred
up, ruffled Lou Emma's blonde braids and Maddy's
dark brown braids. It pinked their cheeks and made
Lou Emma's light blue eyes . . . exactly like her father's . . . and Maddy's dark blue eyes sparkle with
the fun of the morning and the trip in their very own

auto. On a clear stretch of road their father looked back and smiled.

"Kansas agrees with you two. You look pretty as a picture." A rut twisted the steering wheel and he had to face front.

"Are we pretty?" Lou Emma asked Maddy seriously. "Mrs. Doctor Waters said we would be if we had a mother to look after us. She told Ella Johnson's mother, and Ella told me for a Trade Last. It wasn't much of a Trade Last."

"I should hope to kiss a pig, it wasn't," Maddy said. Giving a compliment in order to get one in return was the rage among the girls in Auden. Ella's Trade Last was really a cheat. "What'd you tell her?"

"All I could think of was that Mag Meeker said she'd swap her head for Ella's to get Ella's naturally curly hair. But she wanted to keep her own brains because she didn't think Ella had many."

"You came out even," Maddy said. "But all Mrs. Doctor Waters wants to do is get Papa to marry her old maid sister from Akron."

"Is she the one that brought us gingerbread, and sang alto at church?"

"I thought it was bass," Maddy said.

"Only men sing bass. When ladies sing bass, they call it alto."

The road took a turn for the worse. The Great

Smith jolted from rut to chuck hole and back again. Professor Miller had to slow down. After twenty miles an hour, ten seems like turtles. The sun beat down, hot.

At noon they ate cheese and crackers washed down with red soda pop bought at a crossroads grocery. They bounced, jolted, and rolled through three more towns. Hens squawked and dogs barked and people stared, but the girls no longer cared. Seventy-five miles was *forever*.

Suddenly, in a weedy pasture loomed a sign.

FIVE MILES TO GLORIOSA

Seeing it, Lou Emma felt a knot twist in her stomach. She thought of the people she must meet, and tell that she was very glad . . . ha-ha . . . to be here. They crowded, tall and faceless, into her mind. She leaned over to the front seat.

"Can't we stop and stretch our legs, Papa?"

"A good idea." Professor Miller headed the Great Smith toward the side of the road, under the shade of a tall cottonwood tree. He turned some metal doodads, and a blessed silence descended. A meadowlark whistled, shrill and sweet. Professor Miller looked at his watch. "We've come seventy miles in less than eight hours. Tell me, did you like it?"

"I loved it when we went fast," Maddy said. "When the wind blew my eyelids back."

"I loved it when we went slow," Lou Emma said, "when I could see the flowers in the grass. And I loved the red soda pop."

"Rule Number One is still working, then?" their father asked.

They agreed with enthusiasm. The Miller family had only three Rules, but they were important. Rule Number One was: The Family Sticks Together, No Matter What.

Long ago Professor Miller had explained to the girls that any family should stick together, but a family with only one parent needed to stick together even harder. He showed them the bundle of rods that the Romans called *fasces* and explained how their strength came from being together.

"Now," he said, "go stretch your legs; I'll stretch my head."

He sat on the running board of the Great Smith with one of the textbooks and H-O-G, and started to study. Every day, except Sunday and Christmas, he studied. The girls slipped quietly from the auto.

"Rule Number Two," Lou Emma said to Maddy, "same as always."

Rule Number Two was: Never Interrupt Papa When He's Studying.

Chapter 2

Lou Emma walked over to a patch of bright sunflowers nodding gaily in the breeze. She was about to
pick one when a black and gold bumblebee zoomed
at her. She backed away, and then she saw Maddy
under the tall cottonwood tree, looking it up and
down. Uneasiness filled her. Maddy wouldn't look at
a tree in that measuring kind of way unless she was
going to climb it, and Lou Emma was no tree-climber.

"Dare you," Maddy said.

Lou Emma shook her head.

"Double-dog, never say die, eat fried mice, and
don't ask why, dare you."

Once more Lou Emma shook her head. "Let's get
in the Great Smith and scrooch down and change
our dresses. We're nearly to Gloriosa."

In each suitcase was a brand new dress—pink for
Maddy, blue for Lou Emma—and on each was a note
in Aunt Jesse's handwriting: "To be put on when in
sight of Gloriosa."

"We're not in sight," Maddy said. "Let's climb
the tree."

"Papa wouldn't want us to," Lou Emma said pi-
ously. "And we can't ask him because of Rule Number Two."

"Shoo-fly," Maddy said. "Papa wouldn't care and
you know it. C'mon."

"C'mon where?" Lou Emma dodged.

"C'mon climb the tree. I'll boost you to the first
limb."

"But I said . . ."

"You said to get dressed because we were nearly to
Gloriosa, but Aunt Jesse said we had to be in *sight*.
Well, if we climb the tree maybe we'll be in sight."

Lou Emma felt that she was losing. "We can't get
dressed in the tree."

"Once we've been in sight of Gloriosa we'll come
down and get dressed. C'mon. I'll lean on the tree
and you climb on my back. Watch that snag."

"How'll you get up? There's nobody to boost you."

"You'll reach me down a hand. Honestly, I think
you're scared."

The worst thing about having Maddy for a sister,

Lou Emma thought, was that she could read your mind. Almost. And Lou Emma was scared of high places. Cold-feet, cowardly-calf, scaredy-cat scared. How could she climb what was probably the tallest tree in Kansas? But how could a girl who was twelve admit to her sister, who was only eleven, that she was scared?

"All right. But only to the first limb. Then I'm going back to the Great Smith and get the *Youth's Companion* that you don't know I know you swiped and hid in Topeka. That's the state capital and it's worse to swipe things there."

"How can I swipe what's half mine?" Maddy's voice was muffled as she leaned against the tree trunk. "Aunt Jesse subscribed to it for both of us."

"It's my turn," Lou Emma climbed onto Maddy's back. "It was your turn on the train, but you kept talking to the porter."

"Get up in the tree," Maddy moaned. "You weigh more than the Prodigal Son and the Fatted Calf put together. Hurry!"

"Not yet. I'm not ready."

But up went Maddy's shoulder and Lou Emma scrambled for the limb.

"Pull yourself up," Maddy directed. *"Up."*

Puffing and struggling, Lou Emma hauled herself onto the first limb of the cottonwood tree. She was sure that her stomach was scraped raw by the pull.

"Reach down." Maddy gave a big jump and caught Lou Emma's hand and climbed catlike onto the first limb beside her sister.

"You nearly pulled my arm out of the sprocket," Lou Emma said. "Now sit still. You promised."

"Me? I never promised any such thing. *You* promised. I'm going up."

Already Maddy was peering through the branches to the far heights of the tree. She was on the second limb, the third. Fearfully, Lou Emma climbed after her. Limb by limb they went upward. Maddy stopped, her foot wedged in a forked limb.

"Isn't it fun?" she trilled. "Isn't it fun?"

Below them was the Great Smith. Professor Miller was sitting on the running board. He had never missed them. The green spot by him was H-O-G.

Maddy swayed back and forth as the wind swayed the tree. "Funnnnnn."

Lou Emma quaked. "If I fell I'd break every bone in my body."

"Only the big ones, like arms and legs. Then you could get a wooden leg like Long John Silver in *Treasure Island* and have a parrot on your shoulder."

"I don't want a parrot. I want to go down. C'mon."

"In a minute." The limb trembled as Maddy went higher.

"Stop shaking the tree," Lou Emma begged.

"I'm not shaking the tree. That's the wind."
Maddy slid back to Lou Emma's limb. "Silly, you've
got your eyes shut."

"I'm practicing that piece you made up for me.
'I'm Professor Miller's daughter . . . ha-ha . . .
and I'm very glad to be here.' "

"Your 'ha-ha' is awful. Sounds like Santa Claus in
the Christmas program."

"It sounds awful because I'm stuck in this awful
tree."

"It's not an awful tree; it's a nice tree. Open your
eyes."

Slowly, Lou Emma forced her eyes to open. Maddy
was sitting beside her, feet dangling into empty space.

"Look up, not down," Maddy said.

Once more Lou Emma made herself obey.
Through the twinkling heart-shaped leaves of the
cottonwood tree she found the summer sky.

*It is kind of fun. If Maddy'd only stop jiggling the
limb.*

"The little clouds are like lambs," she said aloud.
"Lambs in a meadow that's blue, not green."

"That big cloud's a wolf," Maddy pointed. "He'll
eat up the lambs."

That was Maddy. Always taking things over.

"You hush. They're my lambs because I made 'em

up. There's no wolf, that's the mother sheep and she'll take care of the lambs. Stop jiggling the limb."

Maddy meant to stop but she could never stay still. The limb jiggled.

"There's the road we came by," Maddy leaned far out and Lou Emma secretly took hold of the edge of her sister's skirt so that she could hold her if she started to fall. "But we're still not in sight of Gloriosa, so we can't put on our new dresses. Why do we have to mind Aunt Jesse when she's in Ohio and we're here?"

"We'd have still been in Ohio if she'd had her way," Lou Emma said.

"Mur-der. She sure tried to get Papa to marry that homely Miss Jenkins."

"I s'pose Miss Jenkins couldn't help her face, but she was so silly. Of all the ones Aunt Jesse tried to marry Papa to, she was the silliest."

"I didn't like any of 'em," Maddy said. "I like things the way they are now. No old stepmother. No old housekeeper. Just Papa and us. U-S, us."

Lou Emma sat very still. She wanted to say that it *might* be nice if their father got married. To have a mother was the thing in the world she wanted most. Couldn't a stepmother be almost the same? But she wasn't going to say it to Maddy. No one could be as *against* things as Maddy.

"Remember how Papa got mad at Aunt Jesse over Miss Jenkins and told her he proposed to bring up his daughters himself, and would she please mind her own business? She had her smelling salts out five times that day."

"I remember," Lou Emma said, wishing she didn't. Quarrels made her sick to her stomach. "I remember when he fired that Mrs. Girty, too."

"All that stuff she told us about we'd burn in hell-fire if we didn't mind her, and I got nightmares and waked up screaming."

"And the one before Mrs. Girty that never made beds till fifteen minutes before Papa came home. And the one before that drank stuff and said it was tonic."

"Mrs. Meally," Maddy said. "I can't remember before her."

"Anyway, Papa's promised no more housekeepers. All we have to do is keep our three Rules." Lou Emma considered. "I'm twelve and you're eleven, so added up that makes twenty-three and that's how old our mother was and she kept house."

"I wonder if the rose-cutting took root," Maddy said.

Lou Emma knew what she meant. They had planted a rose-cutting the week before they left Auden in the cemetery by the headstone marked Elizabeth Thorne Miller, Beloved Wife of Cyrus Harper

Miller. A glass fruit-jar protected it, and Ella Johnson had promised faithfully to water it in the summer.

"I think it'll grow. We soaked it in rainwater from the barrel, and it had mosquito wigglers in it. If they grow then a rose ought to grow."

"It'd better grow," Maddy said crossly. "Or I'll tell Ella to pull it up by the roots. Lou Emma, do you remember our mother?"

"A little. Do you?"

"I don't know." Maddy jerked a piece of bark from the limb. "Sometimes I think I do. Sometimes I think I don't. That's what makes it so awful."

"What I remember is that I fell off the back porch and skinned my knee. Somebody picked me up and kissed the skinned place. She smelled good. Like roses. It was our mother."

"It could've been one of the neighbors. Or a housekeeper."

"No," Lou Emma said. "It was our mother. I don't know how I know, but I just do."

"It's not fair. If you remember, then I ought to."

"I'm a year older. I was four when she died. You were only three."

"It's not *fair*," Maddy said again.

There are times when there is nothing to say. With her heart in her mouth, Lou Emma moved along the jiggling limb to Maddy and put her arm around her.

Presently she said, "Do you believe the world is round? It doesn't look it from here."

"Maybe the world is round, but Kansas is flat," Maddy said.

"Flat as a pancake, flat as a flitter. What's a flitter?"

"I don't know, but Kansas is nice. Looky . . ."

For the first time Lou Emma took a long look at the land below her, stretching away for miles, gently rolling, green with crops and wild grass, studded with trees. Lines of Osage Orange . . . a thorny hedge . . . divided many of the fields. Cloud shadows sailed over. Meadowlarks whistled. The sweet smell of summer was everywhere. A strange, happy feeling came over her.

Maddy jabbed her elbow into Lou Emma's ribs. "Somebody's coming."

Down the straight road, drawn like a pencil mark through the grass, came a shabby buggy pulled by a slew-footed gray mare. It came slowly and stopped beside the Great Smith. Professor Miller kept on reading. Up in the tree the girls knew that he was at least two thousand years back in time. The mare turned her head; her washboard sides heaved.

Then from the rag-tag buggy stepped a young woman dressed in a blue linen coatsuit, elegantly tailored. On her dark hair was a white hat trimmed with three pink roses. A long swathe of white veiling was tied in a bow beneath her chin. She stood, calmly, waiting for Professor Miller to look up.

"She doesn't know Rule Number Two," Maddy giggled.

"Ought we to drop a stick on H-O-G?" Lou Emma asked.

As she spoke Professor Miller looked up. He jumped to his feet and H-O-G spilled from the running board into the dust.

"Do you see what I see?" Maddy spoke, awed.

"Pink roses on her hat?"

"No, H-O-G down in the dirt, and Papa *leaving it lay.*"

Maddy was right. There in the dust was the green-covered *History of Greece* that their father consulted as he said the Greeks consulted the Delphic oracle.

"I'm going down and pick it up." With Maddy, to think was to act.

Lou Emma got hold of one dark braid. "Not now."

"*Leggo!* You've been fussing and fuming to get down from this tree since before we got up. Why don't you want me to go down now?"

"I don't know." There wasn't one sensible reason in Lou Emma's head. But inside her, in a place she thought of as her gizzard, was a feeling stronger than reason. *Don't butt in.* She gave a sharp twist to Maddy's braid. "Look there."

"Ouch! Where?"

When Lou Emma spoke there wasn't a thing to look at. Suddenly, on the long straight road there appeared a high-stepping chestnut horse pulling a surrey with a smart tan top. It must be a miracle. She stared, with Maddy.

"Jerusalem my happy home," Maddy quoted their late housekeeper, Mrs. Girty. "I'd like to know where that came from!"

"Maybe from Gloriosa," Lou Emma guessed.

"Good thing we're up here then. We never did change our dresses."

Lou Emma had a prime chance to say 'I told you so,' but she let it go. Below, the young lady with the pink roses on her hat was getting back into the buggy. Professor Miller, the sun bright on his hair, was pointing her down the road. The road to Gloriosa? Lou Emma could only hope so, not knowing why she cared.

"Look at that horse step," Maddy was watching the oncoming surrey. Lou Emma didn't answer. She was watching the sagging old buggy where a flying end of white veiling fluttered as if it were waving good-bye.

"The surrey's going to stop," Maddy said excitedly. "And I wish you'd look at that fancy laprobe with an initial."

"It's B, the same curly kind as on Barton's Best Baking-powder."

"Papa acts as if he knows 'em. They're getting out."

With a sinking heart Lou Emma said, "It's just come to me. That B on the laprobe—it could be for Biddle. Dr. Amos T. Biddle is the name of the president of Eastern Kansas Classical College."

"There's prob'ly a million B's in Kansas. Take John Brown."

"Not him. His 'body's mould'ring in the grave,' the song says."

"But . . ." Maddy looked down at the people below, then at Lou Emma. "You're right. I'll bet one million dollars that's the Amos T. Biddles. But if you say 'told you we ought to change dresses' I'll kill you every day."

"I won't say it," Lou Emma promised. "But you do look a mess."

"You look like something the cat drug in," Maddy said.

They were both right. Their dresses were wrinkled and grimy, their braids fuzzy, their stockings saggy, and their faces and hands none too clean.

"Lou Emma . . . Maddy . . ." It was their father calling.

"Louisa Emmaline . . . Madeline Margaret . . ." he called again.

"Yes*sir*." They sang it out together. Double names meant double-quick.

On the ground the grownups looked up surprised as the answer floated down from the tall cottonwood. The man took off his black derby hat and held it up to shade his eyes. The woman beside him was taller than he was by six inches. She wore a hat almost as big as one of the wheels of the Great Smith. Every inch of it was smothered in twisted, folded, tormented purple satin.

"Maybe it's not the Biddles, after all," Lou Emma said.

"Those are Biddles if I ever saw Biddles. C'mon, let's get it over." Maddy began her quick, sure, limb-after-limb descent. Lou Emma followed more cautiously, looking down each time to place her foot right. All at once she drew back as if the limb below were red-hot.

"There's a boy down there."

Like a reluctant turtle, a boy was emerging from the surrey.

"Boys aren't poison," Maddy went on down. "Get a wiggle on."

But Lou Emma clasped the tree trunk.

"The longer you wait, the worse it'll be," Maddy whispered upward.

The fear of meeting new people, added to the fact that one of them was a boy, and boys were worse than plain people, froze Lou Emma.

"Rule Number One." Her father's voice was crisp and crackling.

"Wait for me, Maddy. Wait . . . wait . . ."

They never agreed on exactly what happened, but in the next moment Maddy hit the ground with an ear-splitting scream, landing on all fours. Lou Emma fell at the same time but with a loud noise of ripping cloth as her skirt caught on the snag of the cotton-wood tree. The stout hem held and she hung, twisting, a few feet from the ground.

Into the shocked silence, after Maddy's scream died away, Lou Emma heard her own voice, unnaturally loud, saying, "I'm Professor Miller's daughter . . . ha-ha . . . and I'm very glad to be here."

Chapter 3

In a split second Professor Miller had Lou Emma down from the snag and turned her around to meet the Biddles, but it seemed like the longest hour of her life. The boy—Thomas, his mother called him— was grinning till his back teeth showed. She tried to hide her unbleached muslin petticoat that was in full view through her torn skirt.

"Welcome to Gloriosa," Dr. Biddle said. "Glad you dropped in."

Mrs. Biddle frowned. "Thank heaven you weren't seriously injured. I can't say that I approve of tree-climbing for little girls."

"We haven't been little for years," Maddy said. "I'm eleven, an' Lou Emma's twelve. This year we had a birthday party and Lou Emma put gray frosting on the cake. It was supposed to be blue but it turned out gray."

Jolted out of her misery by this unfair report on her cooking, Lou Emma turned on Maddy. "It was your idea in the first place. I told you blue ink would taste awful, and it looked awful, too."

"We'll get right to work to find you a housekeeper," Mrs. Biddle said.

The girls looked at their father.

"Thank you," Professor Miller said, "but the girls look after me and I try to look after them. We've agreed to do without housekeepers for the time."

"Forever," Lou Emma said. "I cook."

"I clean house. I cook when Lou Emma lets me," Maddy said.

"Papa says Maddy's cooking is phe-nom-e-nal; I'm just a plain cook."

Dr. Biddle coughed and choked. Maddy advised him to hold his hands over his head, which he did in the manner of a man used to obeying females.

"I've got a goat," Thomas blurted. "He'll eat anybody's cooking. He ate Pa's boiled shirt right off the line."

"Thomas," the purple satin on the huge hat shook with annoyance, "I have told you repeatedly, that goat must *go*."

"Where'd I get another goat as good as Swish? Why he's just a kid and he can already climb steps, stand on a rollin' keg, chase dogs . . ."

"That will do," Mrs. Biddle said.

Lou Emma looked sympathetically at Thomas. who winked at her. Even his eyelids were freckled. She had never seen such a freckled boy.

He came nearer. "Tommy's my real name. Only Ma calls me Thomas."

"Hello, Tommy," Lou Emma said. The Maltese cat that had to be left in Auden was named Tommy, so she felt at home with the name.

Maddy gave her a nod. "See? Ot-nay oison-pay."

"I know pig Latin, too," Tommy said. "Who's 'not poison?' "

"Quite an auto*m*obile," Dr. Biddle admired the Great Smith. "When you wrote you were driving from Topeka, I frankly doubted you'd make it."

"The Great Smith can go thirty miles an hour," Maddy bragged.

Mrs. Biddle looked alarmed. "I hope you don't plan any such speed in Gloriosa. The city has recently placed a limit of six miles an hour, which is high enough. I really wonder if such an auto*m*obile is the right example for the college students."

"Lavinia, we must keep up with the times," her husband said.

"My father came to Kansas from Ohio in a covered wagon," Mrs. Biddle said.

"My grandfather came to Ohio from Massachusetts on a keelboat," Professor Miller countered. "But I doubt if he would do it today."

Mrs. Biddle looked miffed, and Lou Emma hurriedly asked about the house they were to live in.

"We hoped to have you near us," Mrs. Biddle said. "Unfortunately . . ."

"Humpin'-jumpin'-jackrabbits," Tommy sputtered. "Why, anybody'd rather live where they're going to. Right next door to Wackers'. Hack Wacker's the best fisherman in the county, and they've got four kids and somethin' goin' on every minute."

"Thomas, *Mister* Wacker, please." Mrs. Biddle reproved him and turned back to the others. "The Wackers are good people. Plain but—ah—good. Mr. Wacker is employed by the Santa Fe railroad in some capacity . . ."

"He's a section foreman," Tommy said. His mother ignored him.

"Mrs. Wacker and I attended school together. We don't always see eye-to-eye, but . . ."

"They've got too big a family," Tommy said.

"Thomas!"

"But Ma, when they had Joy you said . . ."

"Get back in that surrey this instant."

"My dear," Dr. Biddle said, "we should be on our return trip. I was about to suggest that we leave Tommy with the Millers to guide them into Gloriosa and their new home."

"Humpin'-jumpin'-jackrabbits." Tommy climbed out of the surrey much faster than he had climbed in. Lou Emma half expected Mrs. Biddle to put an end to such a plan but she nodded majestically.

"Welcome to Kansas, Professor Miller. And to you, my dear little girls." Lou Emma pinched Maddy so that she wouldn't protest that "little girls" again. "We'll expect Thomas later, but not too soon, please."

"No speeding," Professor Miller agreed, helping Mrs. Biddle into the surrey. "Thank you for coming to greet us."

"Ain't she a pill?" Maddy whispered to Lou Emma.

"There ain't no such word as ain't," Lou Emma whispered in return.

"I can drive an auto," Tommy said. "Ma'd have a dozen duck fits if she knew, but I can. Ed Taylor let me drive his Franklin over to the grounds where they're gettin' ready for the Gloriosa Chautauqua Assembly. I drove Jim Murphy's Studebaker Four, too."

They were in the Great Smith, the engine chug-chug-chug-chugging steadily as if the rest had given it new vigor. Maddy was in the center of the back seat, Tommy on the right, Lou Emma on the left. Professor Miller called over his shoulder, "Mind over matter. That's all."

Lou Emma turned back to look at the tall cotton-wood tree. She thought of how the world looked from up there . . . the rolling fields, the dark green hedge, the lamblike clouds.

Goodbye, tree, I had a nice time.

Ahead of them a brown cow appeared in the middle of the road. From the ditch alongside a black-and-white cow joined her. A red cow with a clanging cowbell ambled out of nowhere. Side by side the three strolled on, completely blocking the narrow road.

"Oo-*oo*-gah, oo-*oo*-gah."

Not one of the cows gave ground. A half-grown red calf joined them.

"Look out, you'll hit the cows," Lou Emma cried.

"Look out, Papa, look out," Maddy echoed.

"Whoa! *Whoa!*" Professor Miller strained on the steering wheel as if he held the reins of a runaway horse. "WHOA!"

On hurtled the Great Smith, straight for the broad backs of the cows. More and more cows crowded onto the road. The road was full of bawling, shoving cows. Professor Miller jerked a lever; the Great Smith leaped forward.

"Don't know how to stop. WHOA!"

In one flashing motion Tommy flung himself over the side of the Great Smith, hit the running board standing up, grabbed the emergency brake and pulled.

The brakes screeched. There was a strong smell of burning rubber. The auto veered right and came to a halt a half-inch from the tail of the brown cow.

"Jerusalem my happy home—I'm dead." Maddy slid down the seat.

"Moooooo," the brown cow bawled. "Mooooo-aw, Mooooo-aw."

"Amen," Professor Miller said and took off his goggles.

Tommy climbed back into the back seat.

Tommy's a hero. Lou Emma moved over to sit be-

side him. *A real hero like Horatius at the Bridge, or
the Boy Stood on the Burning Deck.*

"You saved our lives, Tommy." Professor Miller
put out his hand. "Our lives, the cows' lives, and
your own life."

Tommy turned red under his freckles as he shook
hands. "Aw, you'd have got 'er stopped. You got
kind of rattled, that was all."

"A driver has no business getting rattled."

"Papa, you said mind over matter was all there
was to it," Maddy said.

"I did, and I'm a conceited, egotistical, half-baked
nincompoop."

The red cow rubbed her neck against the Great
Smith's headlamps. A swarm of stinging flies buzzed
around the people in the auto.

"It's Garrett's herd," Tommy said. "Must've busted
a fence down the line. Garretts own the land from
here to town, pretty near. They gave the land for the
college."

"I don't care if they gave the whole town the mea-
sles," Maddy slapped at a fly on her arm. "How are
we going to get through that—that mess of cows?"

"I could chase the cows off the road while you
drive," Tommy said to Professor Miller.

"Correction. I chase, you drive."

"Me? Drive the Great Smith?" Tommy whistled.

"You couldn't do worse than I did. I think you'll do better."

By pulling up tall sunflowers to use as switches, by throwing clods, and shouting, "Get along . . . beat it . . . begone . . . vamoose . . ." Professor Miller, Lou Emma, and Maddy cleared the road of cows, but it was a long, tiresome business. They were a half-mile from where they started when they climbed wearily back into the Great Smith and Tommy turned the wheel over to Professor Miller. The sun was low in the west, now, and the white clouds were golden. Flights of birds flocked toward home.

"Wish we were going home. Back to Auden," Maddy said to Lou Emma.

"Me too."

She didn't really want to go back to Auden. She only wanted to go someplace that she knew, and that knew her. In Gloriosa an empty house was waiting. She thought of it, dark, dusty, unfurnished. All their belongings, shipped by freight, would be in some freight house, all higgledy-piggledy.

"Wonder where we'll sleep? Where's our bed?" Maddy said.

"Or the *Lares* and *Penates*." These were the Morris chair and the green-shaded lamp, for their father had told them how the Romans had household gods, and wherever they were these things made *home*.

The Great Smith chugged ahead. The fields gave
place to houses. Here and there lamps were lighted.
Boys and girls played ball in the street.

"Here's Gloriosa," Tommy said.

It was all too new and strange. Lou Emma wanted
terribly to jump out and run, run, run. She tried to
think of something familiar. The kitchen stove. It
was a Wilson's Patent with a bunch of grapes on the
oven door. One leg was broken and propped up by
a brickbat.

Our mother used the stove.

"There's the Assembly Grounds for the Chautauqua. It'll be starting the last two weeks of August.
Everybody goes," Tommy said. "Rent tents and
camp."

"Which way now?" Professor Miller asked.

"Turn left. Third house. William Jennings Bryan's
going to speak."

"My eyes are shut, I won't look," Maddy said.
"Tell me, Lou Emma."

The Great Smith slowed, stopped. "Third house?
But it's occupied."

"Jehosaphat!" Tommy yipped. "But that's the
house. I know it is."

It was a small brown house, its front porch heavy
with honeysuckle. In the fading light they could see
the front door standing open. Lamplight gleamed in

welcome from the windows. Furniture was in the rooms.

"There must be some mistake," Professor Miller said. "Wait here and I'll go and see."

But Lou Emma was running up the sidewalk to the front door. With every step she saw more and more . . . the Morris chair, the green-shaded lamp, the library table, the worn Axminster rug. It was all there. It was *home*.

How it had happened she did not know, but it had happened.

"Shhhh, don't ask questions," she said to the sputtering Maddy, who had caught up with her.

It was the second miracle of the day.

Chapter 4

Lou Emma was awake, but her eyes were closed. She knew it was morning because her eyeballs could tell the difference between daylight and dark. A rooster crowed. Ohio roosters crowed for day, so Kansas roosters must do the same, "Things which are equal to the same things are equal to each other. Euclid."

Beside her, Maddy was sound asleep. Their father said that Maddy could sleep through the Punic Wars. To be awake when somebody in the same bed is asleep is to be stronger, more powerful. Lou Emma kept quiet, enjoying the feeling.

Last night had been a miracle, she decided. Her father said "It must be a mistake," but she knew better. She hadn't tried to explain it because a miracle must be believed, or it will go away and leave no trace, the way a soap bubble bursts.

There was the house, shining with welcome. There were the *Lares* and *Penates*. And as if that were not enough a rich and wonderful smell of food came from the kitchen. On the Wilson's Patent cookstove stood a black kettle and in its depths simmered a beef stew, thick with vegetables, bubbling with gravy. A loaf of home-made bread cooled on a snowy tea towel on the kitchen table. From the dark cave of the oven came the perfume of hot apple pie.

All this, and not a single soul in sight.

"Manna in the wilderness." Professor Miller took off his hat. "Children of Israel, wash your hands."

They took turns washing at the little red-painted iron pump at one end of the zinc-lined sink. Maddy located soup bowls, Lou Emma the spoons and the butcher knife with the black handle. Maddy got "dibs" on the heel of the loaf, and as Professor Miller was slicing it, a pound print of butter appeared on the window sill where Lou Emma swore there was nothing when they came into the kitchen.

They ate the beef stew and mopped up the gravy with chunks of bread slathered with butter. The apple pie was tart and sweet at the same time.

"Lucullus may have eaten better in Rome but I

doubt it." Professor Miller settled back with a sigh of contentment.

At that moment, outside the window where the butter had appeared, they heard a giggle. Then the sound of feet—bare feet—scurrying away.

Maddy jumped up to give chase but her father pulled her back. "If angels want to be unaware, we should let them."

"I only wanted to say 'thank you.' It's polite to be polite to angels."

"Maybe we ought to act as if we didn't hear anything at all," Lou Emma said. "The way we do at Christmas when Aunt Jesse leaves snips of yarn around but we act surprised when she gives us crocheted caps."

"Those horrible-storrible caps," Maddy rolled her eyes upward.

"We don't have to wear 'em, out here in Kansas, do we Papa?"

"Girls," Professor Miller shook his head. "Jesse means well. She just doesn't realize that styles have changed. And it's what's in your head, not on it, that matters."

"If Aunt Jesse means well, why won't she get a stylebook, and make some caps we can wear?" Maddy argued. "Why do we have to be the goat?"

Lou Emma said nothing but she thought Meaning

Well is a thing that grownups have to help each other out. She started scraping the dishes.

"No dishes tonight," Professor Miller ruled. "Get on to bed."

The stairs were like a mountain Lou Emma had to climb. She went up on all fours, like a baby. Her clothes came off in jerks. The only prayer she could think of was "Thank You." Maddy had to pull-haul her into bed.

Once in the night she waked, knowing her father had come in and pulled some cover over them, for the wind was cool. There was something she wanted to tell him, but her mouth was full of cotton-wool and no sound came.

What was it she had tried to say? As the morning light grew brighter, back of her closed eyelids came a dancing image. A white hat with three pink roses. But why should she have wanted to tell her father that? He said only last night it was what was *in* the head that mattered, not what was *on* it. The hat faded but the roses remained, like the grin on the Cheshire Cat in *Alice in Wonderland*.

She blinked her eyes and decided it was time to get up. As she slipped from the bed Maddy rolled into the vacant space, taking two-thirds of the cover. Summer or winter, Maddy was a cover-snatcher.

Dressing quietly, Lou Emma then padded downstairs. The dishes had been washed and the table set
for breakfast but this was no miracle, this was her
father.

Outside the window she heard a giggle, the exact
duplicate of the one she had heard last night. She
pulled open the side door, quickly, and there stood
two girls . . . about the age of the Miller girls . . .
and a boy who was younger. They all three had
red hair. *Not* reddish hair, but fire-red, carrot-red,
copper-milk-pan-in-the-sun red.

"H-hello," Lou Emma said.

"Hello," the bigger of the girls said.

The two "hellos" hung in the air like melting ice-
cream cones. Maddy was not there to take over for
her. Lou Emma struggled alone.

"I guess you're our neighbors," she said.

"We're the neighborest neighbors you got," the
boy said. "Nobody on t'other side and us Wackers
are all on this side till you get to McKelvy's. And
McKelvys don't count 'cause they've got no kids and
skunk-mean besides."

The bigger girl clamped her hand over his mouth
but the boy pried loose her fingers. "Which are you?
The big'un or the little'un?"

It was hard to answer. Maddy was taller but Lou
Emma was older. She dodged the questions. "I'm

Lou Emma and my sister's Maddy. She's asleep. Are you the ones that fixed our house? And our supper?"

"Mama did it mostly," the smaller girl said. "She says to let new neighbors come to an empty house an' no food ready would be heathen."

"It was wonderful," Lou Emma said, and wished there was another, better word. "It was wonderful, multiplied by twelve."

"I peeled the apples for your old pie," the boy said, "only Mama said I et too many and took 'em away. Hoo-hoo, I'm an Indian." He began to run in circles yelling and patting his mouth. "Hoo-hoo-hoo . . ."

That brought Maddy down, and into the yard. "What's going on?"

"This is my sister I told you about," Lou Emma said. "We're Professor Miller's daughters . . ."

"Shoot a mile!" the boy stopped running. "You don't hafta tell us that. Miz Biddle's told everybody in Gloriosa all there is to tell. Hoo-hoo-hoo."

"We know all about Mrs. Biddle but she doesn't know all about us," Maddy retorted, and as usual Lou Emma wished she had thought to say it. "What's your names?"

"I'm Vinnie Wacker," the bigger girl said, "and this is Eppie, and this is our brother Hackberry. His real name's Charles Elgin but he likes Hackberry.

Don't pay any attention to him, or he'll just act worse."

"Hoo-hoo-hoo, I'm an Indian," Hackberry yelled and took off across the yard, suddenly catching at a trapeze bar hanging from a crab-apple tree, skinning the cat, and at last crouching on the bar, like a red-headed monkey.

"Thank goodness he's gone," Eppie said. "Can you play Hopscotch?"

There was a big grassless stretch in the Wacker yard that had been played down to the bare earth. Eppie took Maddy there to the Hopscotch game she had marked out. Vinnie took Lou Emma to the playhouse that was outlined on the ground with rocks and sticks. "Come in," she said politely.

"Thank you very much," Lou Emma gave the proper grownup answer.

A ginger-colored cat strolled over and Vinnie grabbed him.

"This is our cat, Mr. Murphy."

Lou Emma extended a finger, but Mr. Murphy gave a flat-eared snarl.

"Mr. Murphy's a kind of funny name for a cat," she ventured.

"It sure is," Vinnie agreed. "I named him Mr. McKelvy first, because he was so mean. Then Mama wouldn't let me call him that on account of the real

Mr. McKelvy lives next door, and he might suspicion why and be mad."

"Did he get mad?"

"Oh he's mad at us most all the time. It's hard to tell the sep'rate things he's mad at. Mama said I could *think* McKelvy, but *say* Murphy."

"Don't you get mixed up?"

"I'll say I do. When I go to sell eggs to Mr. McKelvy I call him Mr. Murphy, and he gets sore as a boiled owl."

"You ought to sell your eggs to somebody else," Lou Emma said.

"Everybody around here keeps their own hens, except McKelvys. They're so tight they eat every single bite at every meal and don't have any chicken scraps left. Only don't tell I told you."

"You can sell us eggs."

"Good. Our eggs are real fresh," Vinnie said. "And we get double-yolks, too, lots of 'em, and don't charge a bit more."

Mr. Murphy broke away from Vinnie and hid under the porch of the rambling house that looked as if it had forgotten the touch of a paintbrush.

Vinnie looked sidewise at Lou Emma. "See my kitchen stove? That stove-top's genuine marble."

Lou Emma smoothed the creamy slab, set on bricks. "It's nice."

"There's something under it. I'll show you, if you won't tell."

"Not even Maddy?" Lou Emma looked at the Hopscotch game.

"Can you cross your heart for her, too?"

Lou Emma crossed her heart twice, and Vinnie lifted the marble top from the playhouse stove. Under it was a nest of fluffy chicken feathers, and in the center of them was a glass prism. Vinnie handed it to Lou Emma, who held it up to her eyes, and looked toward the sun. Rainbows gleamed, and the world splintered into dancing color. She moved the prism up and down, entranced.

"Where'd you get it?"

"That's the secret," Vinnie lowered her voice. "It came out of a saloon."

Lou Emma's mouth dropped open.

"Uncle Elgin gimme it," Vinnie said. "He was up to Topeka and he'd just stepped inside this saloon to get a little something to take care of a cold he felt coming on when . . . slam-bang . . . here came Carry Nation, and a lot of other ladies with hatchets and stuff and they wrecked the saloon."

"But how'd he get the prism?"

"It was part of a big hanging lamp and Uncle Elgin said Carry Nation, herself, personally, knocked it down. So he picked up this prism because it was kind of *historic*. Only he told me not to tell Mama where it came from or she'd never in the world let me keep it."

"Did your Uncle Elgin get over his cold?"

"He said it was scared out of him, but it comes back now'n' then."

"Carry Nation's pretty brave," Lou Emma said.

"She sure is. She's real brave against the Demon Rum. And she's against tobacco, too. She's death on cigarettes."

Red, blue, violet glints from the prism danced on Lou Emma's skirt. Part of her thrilled to Carry Nation's bravery, but part of her wished that the lamp was in one piece and she might see it with all prisms flashing.

"I'm not going to tell Maddy," she said to Vinnie. "If I told her, and showed her the prism, she'd decide to do just like Carry Nation."

"There's not any saloons in Gloriosa. Not with prisms, anyway."

"There weren't any aer-o-planes in Auden when the Wright brothers at Dayton invented one, but that didn't keep Maddy from jumping out of the hayloft with a pair of wings she made."

"Did she get hurt?"

"I did," Lou Emma said. "She fell on me and broke my collar-bone."

Vinnie covered the prism with feathers and put the marble top back on the stove. "You can look at it whenever you want to."

"Here comes Mama with Joy," Eppie shouted and gave a mighty hop that carried her outside the Hopscotch game. Vinnie scrambled after her. Mr. Murphy came out from under the steps. Hackberry chinned himself on the trapeze bar.

"Looky at me, Mama, looky at me, looky . . ." he yelled.

As if by common consent Lou Emma and Maddy moved toward each other, their shoulders touching. Mr. Murphy rubbed against Lou Emma's ankles and she scooped him up, grateful for his attention. Other girls' mothers sometimes liked her and sometimes didn't, *but they always liked their own girls the best.*

Mrs. Wacker came right over to the Miller girls and hugged them. "I'm *that* glad to see you. Hackberry, be quiet . . . *be quiet* . . . for one minute."

"I AM QUIET, MAMA. LOOKY HOW I CAN CHIN MYSELF."

"That boy!" Mrs. Wacker said. "But if he was quiet I'd be callin' the doctor. We're tickled pink you've come to be neighbors to us, and that means Mr. Wacker, too, only he's gone fishing this morning."

She stood beaming at them. She was a short, stout

woman, made like a sofa pillow tied in the middle. She wore a blue calico dress, faded after many washings. The hair that straggled out from her dustcap was unmistakably red, though it, like the dress, was faded. Looking at her Lou Emma knew that this was a person she need have no fear of meeting. A warm, letting-go feeling came over her and she forgot about her memorized piece.

The Miller girls began thanking her for all she had done, but she waved them away with a plump hand.

"It wasn't such-a-much. We were just doin' unto others, you know." She took baby Joy's small soft hand and patted Lou Emma's cheek with it. Joy was chubby with red hair like the others. Lou Emma remembered what Tommy had said and wondered what Mrs. Biddle could mean. Surely, anybody would want a darling baby like Joy.

"All of us pitched in to help," Eppie said. "The hardest part was getting Mr. Deatherage at the depot to bring your furniture before you came."

"The fuss he made," Mrs. Wacker laughed and Joy crowed with delight. "Said there wasn't any rule in the railroad rule book for such's that."

"And Mama said, 'Didn't you never hear of the Golden Rule? It's older'n the Santa Fee.'" Vinnie reported proudly.

"Mr. Wacker convinced him. Workin' for the Santa Fee, himself, and then him and Joe Deatherage soldiered together in the Philippines. Two men that's drunk from the same canteen'll do plenty for each other."

"Has the Professor read all those old books we un-loaded?" Hackberry demanded. "Every single page? Without skippin'?"

"Worse'n that," Maddy said. "Some twice."

"Think of it," Mrs. Wacker marveled. "Here I don't get the *Household* read, half the time. Good mornin' Professor, we're glad you're here."

Professor Miller had crossed the yard without the girls knowing it. Lou Emma felt a twinge of pride in his good looks, and his—niceness. He thanked Mrs. Wacker for her help, chucked Joy under the chin, admired Vinnie's playhouse, bragged on Eppie's Hop-scotch game, and shook hands with Hackberry.

"I'm glad to see another man around," he said.

"And I'm glad that red auto's next door," Hack-berry said. "Nobody in Gloriosa's got one like that. Not Mr. Garrett that owns half the county, nor Mosses that run th' ice 'n' coal, nor Strunks to the bank. Or old Miz Bossy B. Biddle."

"Miz Biddle said right to Mama's face that we had no business with another baby when Joy was born," Vinnie's eyes were round and blue.

"Vinnie, go wash the breakfast dishes. Eppie, give Joy her bottle. Hackberry, get after the weeds in the onion bed. *Scat.*" Mrs. Wacker slapped her hands and the young Wackers vanished like magic. Even Mr. Murphy disappeared.

"Excuse us, Professor," Mrs. Wacker's face was pink. "I don't hold malice against Lavinia Biddle. She 'n' I lived south of town as girls. Went to the same country school. Our folks got grasshoppered out the same year. She's bossy as a hen with one chick, but I'll give her good for one thing—nobody works as hard for the college as Lavinia."

"I'm sure you're right," Professor Miller smiled. "Girls, breakfast."

Chapter 5

Breakfast was over and the oatmeal pan was washed. Every morning the oatmeal pan stood between Lou Emma and freedom. Once it was scrubbed clean, dried, and put back into the fireless cooker, her day could begin. Maddy washed dishes every other day, but more often than not she hid the oatmeal pan, or left it to soak, or put it on top of the stove where scraps of oatmeal dried into a cementlike crust. Professor Miller believed in oatmeal for breakfast the way he believed in learning Latin. Both provided a firm foundation for whatever might come later.

"We'll go to see the college when you're ready,"

he said as Lou Emma draped the tea towel over the dishpan. "I have some reading to do. Call me."

"We'd better put on our new dresses," Lou Emma said to Maddy. "Goodness knows, we're in sight of Gloriosa, or it's in sight of us."

Maddy tossed her braids. "I'm going to Wackers' and play Hopscotch."

Out she skipped, leaving her sister cross as two sticks.

Going up to get dressed Lou Emma kicked every other stair tread. It hurt her big toe, but it helped her feelings. She hated to be "the good one," always to do what her father said and try to get Maddy to do it too.

It's not fair. Just because I'm the oldest. Half the time Papa's nose is in a book and he doesn't know what goes on. If he'd just get married . . .

Her new dress was wrinkled and ought to be pressed, but the fire in the kitchen stove was out, and it took a long time to heat the sad-irons. Better to wear it unpressed. She put it on, trying to smooth the wrinkles with her hands.

Maddy came tearing upstairs, grabbed her new pink dress and ran down. Lou Emma watched as she raced across the yards, jumping the straggling line of dark red Prince's Feather that divided them, going into Wackers' door.

She went on with her own dressing, washing her feet in the big china bowl, putting on clean white stockings, rubbing Vaseline on her patent leather slippers. What was going on over there?

Maddy came bouncing back in the pink dress, every wrinkle ironed out, her dark hair brushed to shining satin. "Mrs. Wacker was doing some ironing so I asked her to do up my dress. And Vinnie brushed my hair."

Bitterness rose in Lou Emma. She tried to do right and things went wrong. Not only this morning, but a million things before, reaching back to the day in Auden after their mother died when their father said, "Look after Maddy, Lou Emma. You're the old-est. I depend on you."

How many times had Maddy run away and hidden and left her sister trudging from house to house look-ing for her? How many times had she concocted schemes that backfired and left Lou Emma in trou-ble? How many times had Maddy traded turns, and then insisted on having her own turn anyway?

It's not fair.

"You're buttoned wrong," Maddy said. "Turn around and let me . . ."

"Mind your buttons and I'll mind mine," Lou Emma said sharply.

"Of all the snippy . . ."

"Oo-*oo*-gah."

Maddy grabbed a pair of clean stockings and ran downstairs. When Lou Emma got into the front seat of the Great Smith she was putting them on.

And she hadn't washed her feet.

Lou Emma bit her lip. The only worse thing than putting clean stockings on unwashed feet was being a tattletale.

"I beat Eppie at Hopscotch," Maddy bragged. "I beat her three times."

"I saw you," Lou Emma said. "She felt terrible, the way you acted."

"I can't help it if I'm a better player. If I didn't beat her when I could, it would be same as cheating, wouldn't it, Papa?"

But Professor Miller was concentrating on starting the Great Smith into motion. Slowly the auto began to roll. Hackberry cheered from the trapeze bar.

"Spark. Gas. Brake. So far so good," Professor Miller muttered. "There are all kinds of ways to win in games. You have to choose your way."

"But I can't help it if . . ." Maddy started. Then she said more slowly, "Maybe I could've. Been nicer, I mean. Not beat her so bad."

The knot of anger within Lou Emma untangled. She gave her sister a quick squeeze. Nobody could stay mad at Maddy long.

Eastern Kansas Classical College was the pride of Gloriosa. Last year it had a student body of seventy-eight, always spoken of as "about a hundred." It had a football team that had beaten its rival, Grandville Teachers. It had a silver loving cup for debate won from the University of Kansas at nearby Lawrence. It had a Glee Club and a Quartet and two secret societies, Chrystomatheon and Golden Bison. With the coming of Professor Cyrus Miller it had a full-time faculty of ten men and women.

The ten-acre campus, given by Mr. Garrett, was on the south edge of town. The upward slope of the ground had inspired the college song, *From Thy High and Lofty Hillside.* Elm saplings lined the driveway. The college was housed in one large cut-limestone building three stories tall, with a belfry on top and a big iron bell; this building was known as Old Main. Beside it was a flat-roofed frame building called Rehearsal Hall that served as chapel, gymnasium, auditorium, and practice room for the Glee Club.

The Great Smith rolled up the driveway. Professor Miller set the brake and turned to his daughters. "We've been skipping your Latin lessons lately. Here's something for you to remember: *Ad astra per aspera.*"

"*Ad astra,* to the stars," Lou Emma translated.

". . . *per aspera*," Maddy frowned. "I think it means 'through hard ways.' But how'd you get to the stars through hard ways? Why'd you tell it to us?"

"It's the motto of the state of Kansas, girls. The more we live here the better we'll understand it. *Ad astra per aspera*," he repeated.

Lou Emma whispered it to herself. "To the stars" lifted her up, but "through hard ways" set her down on solid earth. It was a good combination.

In the office with PRESIDENT on the door, Dr. Biddle seemed taller than when the girls had looked down on him from the cottonwood tree. Or was it only the absence of Mrs. Biddle and the purple hat? He listened, nodding, to their story of the Wackers' welcome.

"Tommy told us, and we thought that might be who it was. A kinder woman never lived than Jane Wacker. She's had a hard time, but you'll never hear that from her. I'm glad they're your neighbors."

"We haven't seen Mr. Wacker," Maddy said.

"No, Hack would be fishing on a day like this." Dr. Biddle glanced out the window as if he would like to be fishing himself. "Now, Professor Miller, what textbooks do you plan to use?"

Professor Miller cleared his throat. "In regard to textbooks . . ."

Maddy and Lou Emma oozed quietly out of the office.

"Let's go see the college on our own," Lou Emma suggested. "If we wait for Papa we'll be old enough to enroll. Let's guess the rooms. That's the Library across the hall."

"Pooh, the books are in plain sight. Next to it is English Lit."

"Pooh for you. It's got the same old statue of William Shakespeare as the one in Auden had. Nose busted, too. I wonder if Shakespeare had a busted nose, or if somebody goes around and busts noses on statues?"

They walked down the hall, their voices getting lower. A school building in summer—grade school or college—is spooky. As if ghosts of long-gone teachers and students are standing around waiting and watching.

Outside a room with a chart of German verbs on the wall, Lou Emma stopped, her head turned, listening. "They're coming."

"Who?" Maddy whispered.

"The Creepers." Her voice was low and chilling.

"Are they for us or against us?"

Once more Lou Emma listened. The floor creaked. "They're for us."

It was a game they had played as long as they could

remember: a private game; never played when other girls were with them, or a housekeeper, or even their father. The Creepers could appear anywhere. Exactly what they were was never certain. They went on all fours and they could go through anything—walls, doors, screens, fire, water. If The Creepers were *for* them, the Miller girls must leave a plainly marked trail. If The Creepers were *against* them, then they must hide every sign of their flight. What happened if The Creepers ever caught them was too horrible to talk about. The girl who first sensed that The Creepers were coming got to say if they were *for* or *against*.

"How'd they get to Kansas?" Maddy asked.

"They have their ways," Lou Emma said. "Now, let's mark our trail."

They tiptoed to the Library. Maddy turned every tenth book on the shelves upside down. Lou Emma took the big dictionary and opened it to the picture of a rattlesnake's fangs. It was the kind of thing The Creepers would like. In English Lit. they perched a paper hat on Shakespeare's head. In German I and II they drew a skull and crossbones on the blackboard. In chemistry a faintly evil odor hung in the air. Maddy sniffed.

"The Creepers have been here already. Let's get upstairs."

They ran up the steps, followed by the ghostly sound of their own footsteps. It was morning, but a shadowy dimness lurked in the corners.

"There's History, where Papa said it would be. We'd better leave a plain sign there or The Creepers will think we're partial to Papa."

"They'll grind his bones to make their bread," Maddy whispered with a hiss.

A map of the Roman world was on the wall. Twenty chairs, in four rows of five, stood before a kneehole desk.

"Let's make it all backwards," Lou Emma said. They turned every chair around, facing the back of the room. The teacher's desk looked forlorn, forgotten.

"Pull down the shades," Maddy said. But before they could do it the sound of something coming upstairs shocked them into silence.

Slippy-slop, slippy-slop, bump, bump, bump.

"D-d-d-don't be sc-sc-scared," Lou Emma trembled. "They're *for* us."

"I wish we'd never made'em up," Maddy moaned.

Slippy-slop, slippy-slop, bump, bump, *bump*.

Whatever it was was right outside the door of History.

"Under Papa's desk," Lou Emma said. She and Maddy huddled together.

Slippy-slop, slippy-slop . . . then a voice, cranky but human.

"Who in the world left these chairs this way?"

Maddy nudged Lou Emma. "We'd better come out. We'll be caught anyway."

"Uh-huh," Lou Emma agreed. "But I'd rather it'd been The Creepers."

"One, two, three," Maddy counted. On the count of three they crawled out and stood up as quickly as possible, trying to look as if huddling under desks was a regular pastime with them.

"Good morning, Mrs. Biddle," they said in chorus.

Whirling around, Mrs. Biddle overturned two chairs. Maddy rushed to pick up one, Lou Emma the other. Mrs. Biddle looked an absolute sight. She wore

an old black-and-white-checked gingham dress with the skirt pinned up around her knees. Her hair was swathed in a ragged towel. On the floor was a bucket of water . . . bump, bump, bump. Near it was a long-tailed wet mop . . . slippy-slop, slippy-slop.

"The Miller girls!" Mrs. Biddle put her hand up to the ragged towel. "Where did you come from?"

There are times when it's better not to tell grown-ups just what they ask. Maddy dodged, but managed to tell the truth.

"Papa brought us up to see the college."

"It's a real nice college," Lou Emma ventured.

"We think it's every bit as nice as Auden College." Maddy grew bolder.

Mrs. Biddle thawed a little, then she frowned, "I'm sure that the wife of the president of Auden College doesn't have to scrub the floors."

Lou Emma struggled for the right thing to say. Out of the blue came the Latin words her father had taught them. *"Ad astra per aspera."*

It must have been the right thing, for Mrs. Biddle smiled.

"Well, honest work never hurt anyone." She poured washing powder into the bucket of water and stirred it to a whirlpool. "Dr. Biddle would turn off the janitor for the summer. He put our cows on the campus to keep down the grass and said the inside didn't need cleaning until just before the Fall term. I know he did it to save money and buy books for the Library, but it provokes me."

"Papa's just the same," Maddy said. "One time we had to wear winter coats 'way too short because he got a book catalog in November."

"The roof leaked three months the year he bought the big dictionary."

Mrs. Biddle poured in more washing powder. "When I heard that the new History professor was coming I decided to scrub his room myself. I couldn't stand for him to think our college had dirty floors."

Lou Emma remembered that Mrs. Wacker said, "Lavinia Biddle works harder for the college than anybody."

"Papa wouldn't know if the floor was scrubbed or not."

"I suppose he wouldn't," Mrs. Biddle sighed. "But I would, and that's what counts. I'll just get these chairs and the desk out and scrub."

"I could help," Lou Emma said. "I'm a good scrubber."

"Me too," Maddy said. "I tie rags to my feet and pretend to roller skate."

"No, no, you girls are all dressed up. And besides you have enough scrubbing to do at home."

"We don't scrub every week," Lou Emma confided. "We wait till it gets real dirty, then it seems as if we've done a big job."

Before Mrs. Biddle's shocked look they retreated to the hall.

"Now why'd you say that?" Maddy scowled at Lou Emma. "It's none of her beeswax when we scrub."

"I know," Lou Emma sighed. "But for a while she was so sociable that I forgot she was Mrs. Biddle."

"No use crying over spilt milk. What about The Creepers?"

Lou Emma listened intently. "They've gone. The Creepers don't like it when we let grownups come around. Next time they'll very likely be *against* us."

Chapter 6

The Millers went on to town to buy groceries. The main street of Gloriosa was Assembly Avenue. It was a wide street, its three business blocks paved with concrete. This gave it a big-citified air. But the hitching racks still stood in front of the stores, and today they were crowded. A few autos could be seen— a Maxwell, a Franklin, a Moon. By far the showiest, shiniest, most elegant of them all was the Great Smith from Topeka. Heads turned as Professor Miller drove slowly along.

Across Assembly Avenue fluttered a cloth banner announcing: GLORIOSA CHAUTAUQUA ASSEMBLY. Others signs read, RENT A TENT. ATTEND EVERY SESSION. BE A BOOSTER. BUY A SEASON TICKET.

Chautauqua was an American institution in 1909. Years ago, in New York State, it had started on the shores of Lake Chautauqua, a combination of Bible study, classes, sociability, and camping out. The movement spread across the country. Tent cities sprang up in groves, beside lakes or streams. Famous orators came to them, scientists, musicians, reformers, humorists, orchestras, dramatic readers. Families came from miles around and camped out. Railroads ran excursion trains. Kansas had been the first state to take up Chautauqua, after New York. There were many Chautauqua encampments in Ohio, but Professor Miller always taught in the summer Teachers Institutes and the girls had never attended. This year they were determined to go.

"Can we go, Papa? I mean may we?" Lou Emma wheedled.

"It's educational," Maddy was sure this was the magic word. "Don't you want us to be educated?"

"In moderation," their father said. "Where shall I leave this auto? Towns ought to provide a place like the old wagon yards."

"Tommy said William Jennings Bryan is going to speak," Lou Emma said.

"Aunt Jesse said everybody ought to hear him, but nobody ought to vote for him," Maddy said. "Why'd she say that?"

"I'm afraid your Aunt Jesse only trusts Ohio politicians with the presidency."

"When I grow up I'm going to be a Suffragette and vote," Maddy said.

"I'm not. I'd be scared to vote," Lou Emma said.

"Don't worry. I'll tell you how. Rule Number One," Maddy said.

"There's a place." Professor Miller angled the Great Smith toward the sidewalk. "Mind over matter. Seems like a long time since I said that. Now let's go to the Big Dollar that Mrs. Wacker recommended and fill our bare cupboard."

It took a long time for the clerk to fill the order Professor Miller had written out. Then he said he wanted to go to the bank and the postoffice. The girls wandered out onto Assembly Avenue to do some exploring, promising to listen for the Great Smith's horn.

Just outside the Big Dollar Lou Emma saw a shiny new penny on the sidewalk. "A lucky penny!"

"How'd you know it's lucky?" Maddy asked grudgingly.

"Any penny you find is lucky." Lou Emma took off her slipper and put the penny under the lining. She stamped her foot and felt it, round and firm, under her heel. "Wish I might, wish I may, get the wish, I wish today."

"You made that up out of 'Star light, star bright,' "
Maddy said. "Made up things won't make wishes
come true."

"They were all made up by somebody, might as
well be me," Lou Emma said.

"What'd you wish?"

*"Ask me no questions, I'll tell you no lies,
Whether I like custard or green apple pies."*

"Stop it!" Maddy stamped her foot. "Tell me what
you wished?"

"Nope."

"A bicycle? A pink brush and comb?"

Lou Emma shook her head till she set her braids
to swinging.

"That wish stuff is just stuff," Maddy said. "Ella
Johnson stamped five thousand white horses to get
a Japanese kimono and she got a flannelette night-
gown."

"Ella couldn't even count to five thousand."

"Her mother got mad and said plenty of girls loved
flannelette gowns."

"Not me," Lou Emma said. "They itch me."

"I'll help you wish if it's a lawn swing," Maddy
said.

"You said wishes were just stuff."

"Maybe so, maybe not. A gold bracelet?"

They had walked down from the Big Dollar as far as the newspaper office of the Gloriosa *Silver Bugle*. Maddy kept guessing, but Lou Emma would not answer. Maddy was too good a guesser.

Above all, Lou Emma did not want Maddy to guess the thing she always wished for . . . on red birds, first stars, new moons, loads of hay, or lucky pennies . . . that their father would marry so they could have a mother.

Somebody to take care of us and belong to us. Even to spank us.

"A silver heart on a chain?" Maddy guessed wildly.

"Save your breath. What's in here?"

The little store building next to the *Silver Bugle* appeared to be empty but the door was ajar. Curiously, Maddy pushed her way in; Lou Emma followed. The windows were dusty, the floor covered with dingy linoleum, gray paint blistered off the walls. But right in the middle of the dreariness stood a small table, and on it was a hat-stand, and on the hat-stand a white hat with three pink roses. White veiling trailed to the table-top.

"It can't be," Maddy said firmly. "It cannot be the same hat."

"It is," Lou Emma said with equal firmness. "I'd know it in the middle of the Sarah Desert."

"I s'pose you mean the Sa*h*arah Desert. But there

could be a thousand white hats in Kansas. Pink roses on 'em, too."

"It's the same hat," Lou Emma said stubbornly.

She knew because it was the third miracle. Miracles always happen in threes. Story books bear that out, time and again. The king has three sons, the princess gets three wishes, the third time's a charm.

"I'm going to try it on," Maddy said.

"No!" Lou Emma couldn't have been more shocked if Maddy had said she was going barefoot to Sunday School.

"Watch me."

Maddy lifted the lovely creation from the hat-stand. She held it high, tilting it this way and that. "It's more your style. You try it on."

Before Lou Emma could stop her, Maddy placed the hat on her sister's head.

As she stood in the dingy room, the white hat resting lightly on her blonde head, a teasing memory came to Lou Emma. Backward and forward it danced, now here, now there. She drew in a deep breath and knew that she smelled the scent of roses. Where had she smelled it before?

"Welcome to my first customers."

The Miller girls jumped. From the back of the store-room came a young woman, her arms piled with boxes. She was dark, slender, tall, and her face was

streaked with dust and perspiration. Her soft brown hair was escaping its hairpins in little curls. As one tickled her forehead she blew it back impatiently. Brown eyes framed by dark lashes smiled at the girls.

"H-hello ma'am," Maddy said, taken off balance.

"We're Professor Miller's daughters," Lou Emma started, and recalling the hat on her head promptly forgot the rest.

The young woman put the boxes on the floor and looked at them curiously. "Miller? I met a man yesterday whose name was Miller. Tall, handsome . . ." Her cheeks turned pink and she moved the boxes with her foot.

"It was Papa," Maddy said. "And we were up in the tree. That's where we saw your hat."

"Here 'tis," Lou Emma held out the hat, careful not to let the veiling brush the dirty floor. "I know I shouldn't've tried it on."

"I put it on her head," Maddy explained. "She couldn't help it."

"Hats in a millinery shop are there to try on." The young woman smiled and put the hat back on the stand. "And this is my millinery shop, or it will be when I get it cleaned up. I'm Kate Turner from Highbank, and I'm going to call my shop Miss Kate's Chapeaux. Do you like that?"

"Sure we do," Maddy said. "What does it mean?"

"*Chapeaux* is French for hats. Kate's such a dumpy name I thought I'd try to give it some zip."

"It's a good name for a millinery shop," Lou Emma said. "But I don't think Kate's a dumpy name. My name's Lou Emma, and my sister's is Maddy."

"We just got to Gloriosa," Maddy said. "We don't know a soul but Biddles, Wackers, and some cows of Mr. Garrett's."

"And Mr. Murphy. He's a cat," Lou Emma said, and added, "Miss Kate."

"You're better off than I am," Miss Kate said. "I don't even know a cat. My family thinks I'm crazy to leave a good business in Highbank and open a shop in Gloriosa where I don't know anybody."

"You know Papa and us," Lou Emma said. "We're not much but we're some."

"That's right," Miss Kate agreed. "Maybe you'll bring your mother to look at my hats."

There it was. It always went the same way. When they met new people it had to be explained all over that the Miller girls' mother was dead, and right away they were treated different from other girls. Lou Emma looked at Maddy and gave the smallest nod for her sister to go ahead and talk.

"Our mother's dead. She died a long time ago. We keep house for Papa ourselves. Since summer started in Auden, and from now on in Gloriosa."

"Well," Miss Kate said briskly, "I think you're pretty smart girls to do all that."

It doesn't make any difference to her, Lou Emma marveled. *She didn't get weepy, or say she was sorry, or call us poor little motherless anythings.*

Maddy galloped ahead. "Aunt Jesse, that's our father's only sister that lives in Cleveland, says Papa ought to get married. But he said he was going to bring us up himself. For better or for worse. Papa wouldn't marry the Queen of England."

"I should think not. The King wouldn't like it," Miss Kate said.

"Well, Aunt Jesse's always bringing out these old maids for him to marry. Horrible-storrible old maids."

"Oh come now," Miss Kate laughed. "Not all old maids are horrible. I'm twenty-six, so I'm an old maid and I ought to know."

"You should've seen Miss Jenkins," Maddy said. "She wanted to put us on a *schedule.* That means no surprises at all. Every day we'd know what was going to happen."

"A schedule with surprises in it might be fun," Lou Emma said. Maddy glared at her but Miss Kate nodded.

"I'd never get my hats made without a schedule. But let's talk about the new stock I have for the shop.

Here." She opened a box and took out a red taffeta tam-o'-shanter and placed it on Maddy's head. Then she found a wide-brimmed Leghorn with pink velvet streamers and a wreath of pink daisies for Lou Emma. She unearthed a looking glass and held it up for them to see.

Lou Emma stared at her face. *Aunt Jesse says "Pretty is as pretty does," but it's not so. I'm pretty. Really and truly.* It was an astonishing thought. She looked at her sister with the red silk on top of her satiny dark hair. *And Maddy, too. Prettier'n me.*

Maddy's eyes were wide. "I never thought hats were so much before."

"Hats are important because people look at your face, first," Miss Kate said. "They are part of the first impression you make. I'll show you . . ."

But outside the Great Smith called, "Oo-*oo*-gah."

"Papa!" Maddy jerked off the red tam and ran. Lou Emma handed the Leghorn hat to Miss Kate. Then to her own astonishment she added a quick hug before she ran after Maddy.

"Making hats?" Professor Miller said. "That attractive young woman wastes her time putting ribbons off and on hats?"

"Hats are important," Maddy said hotly.

"People look at your face first," Lou Emma said. "First impressions . . ."

"Decorate the inside of your heads, not the outside, and you won't have to worry about first impressions," Professor Miller said. "Study Latin. Read Gibbon's *Decline and Fall of the Roman Empire.* Try some Shakespeare. Forget hats."

"The tam-o'-shanter has a red tassel on top," Maddy said.

"There was some little tiny golden wheat down in the daisies," Lou Emma said. "And the velvet streamers came clear to my waist."

"Hats have gone to your head," Professor Miller said disgustedly. He drove along Assembly Avenue behind Moss's ice wagon. "Look who's here . . ."

It was Tommy and his gang, hanging onto the back steps of the ice wagon, sucking chips of ice. Inside the wagon great cakes of ice smoked in the heat. Ice tongs rattled. Tommy waved and the Miller girls waved back.

As short a time as two days ago Lou Emma knew she would never have waved at a boy . . . no matter what Maddy did. Now she waved at Tommy's gang who were whooping and hollering at the Great Smith. A girl who has just seen herself wearing a Leghorn hat with pink velvet streamers doesn't need to be so afraid of boys.

Vinnie brought over a panful of green beans from the garden for their supper. As she snapped them,

Lou Emma thought about Miss Kate Turner, and the millinery shop, and the wonder of the third miracle. She sliced some salt pork to cook with the green beans and nearly lost a finger to the black-handled knife.

"Look out," Professor Miller shouted as he came into the kitchen. "I've never seen a female who could handle a sharp knife properly. About those hats . . . maybe they are more important than I thought. We'll have to see about getting you girls some new things to wear."

Lou Emma hugged him, hard, and he went away saying she had broken his ribs. As she added salt to the beans and watched it dissolve something suddenly came clear to her.

The scent of roses that lingered around the white hat in Miss Kate's millinery shop was the same scent she remembered from the time her mother had picked her up and kissed her skinned knee when she was four years old.

"Papa," she called, intending to ask him. But she heard the creak of the Morris chair and knew he had settled himself to study. Rule Number Two, she reminded herself.

But she didn't need to ask him, really. She didn't need to ask anyone if this was the same scent.

She knew.

Chapter 7

The first two weeks in Gloriosa fairly flew. Professor Miller had to be at the college, which the girls learned to call EKCC, and they were left on their own.

They learned the ways of the small brown house: its secret cubbyholes, which windows had to be propped up, where the hooks were too high or too low for their belongings, and which was the best place to catch the night breeze at bedtime. They explored the fruit cellar with its chill, earthy smell and looked at the ancient jars of home-canned fruit, long ago forgotten and turned brown. They shouted down the cistern and heard the wavery echoes of their voices returned.

Behind the house was a little barn that had been unused for years. Dusty old hay was still stored there.

The Great Smith was kept in the barn and gradually the smell of gasoline and oil was overcoming the smell of long vanished cows, hay, and bran. A grape arbor with heavy unpruned vines and bunches of purpling Concord grapes was between the house and the barn.

The best thing about the house was the way the work could be left undone without showing, much. "It's a lick'n' a promise house," Maddy said, sweeping dust into a crack in the kitchen floor. Lou Emma agreed and wondered if they had to hang the lace curtains from Auden in the front room.

"Curtains are dustcatchers. Do we have to hang 'em?"

"Rule Number Three," Maddy said.

Rule Number Three was: Keep Clean, Keep Fed, Keep Happy. Anything else is Fancywork.

By applying this Rule the bare bones of the housework were done before ten in the morning. That left Maddy free to join Eppie and Hackberry, who were digging a cave in the vacant lot. Lou Emma and Vinnie had changed the playhouse into a millinery shop and were busy trimming hats with chicken feathers.

Professor Miller came home for dinner at noon, helped with the cooking and the washing up and then went back to EKCC. The afternoon was a lazy time for the girls when they made a pallet on the grass and took naps, or read, or stared up at the sky.

They were doing just that when Maddy rolled over and suggested that they open a lemonade stand, using the lemonade in the ice-box.

"That lemonade's for callers, and you know it," Lou Emma said.

Gloriosa was a formal town. Calls on new families were part of the ritual, and the lack of a mother didn't free the Miller girls from the responsibility of receiving them. The little sandalwood tray in the front room was already full of engraved calling cards, left by hatted, gloved ladies dressed in filmy summer finery. Mrs. Wacker advised the girls to keep a pitcher of lemonade ready to serve at all times.

"I'm tired of callers." Maddy rolled to the edge of the pallet. "They all came from Ohio, and they act as though that was the cream on the clabber. Shoot, we came from Ohio, too, and we don't act that way."

"Papa said Ohio and Kansas had special ties on account of the Civil War. Don't forget, Grandpa Miller was Captain Morgan Miller of the Union Army and Papa said that was something to be proud of."

"I'm proud of Grandpa Miller, I just don't want to hear about him all the time." Maddy came up from the pallet, uncrossing her feet.

"Let's go drink up the lemonade in the ice-box and make some fresh," Lou Emma said. "When that

Mrs. Moss came to call we didn't have a cold drink to give her and I think she thought we ought to buy more ice from her husband."

"We should've given her the cold shoulder," Maddy said. "She gave me the pip."

Maddy measured out sugar and water while Lou Emma rolled the lemons. They turned squishy under her hands.

"If Papa'd get married there'd be somebody besides us to sit and listen to callers." A lemon burst open and juice squirted. "If we had a mother . . ."

"Stupid," Maddy banged the cover of the sugar bin. "We would not have a mother. We'd have a stepmother. You know about them. They're in all the books."

Lou Emma licked the lemon juice from her fingers and wished she had kept her mouth shut. All the story-books had wicked stepmothers. There had to be some nice ones somewhere. She tried to think of the right thing to say to squelch Maddy, but Maddy left and went over to Wackers'.

Lou Emma finished making the lemonade and got down the glass pitcher from the top shelf. Her mother had bought the pitcher in Cincinnati. If she had bought it, she must have handled it. Lou Emma traced the curving line of the fern cut into the glass. Maybe her mother had done the same.

Maddy and the three Wackers had gone before Lou Emma went over to join them. Mrs. Wacker was sitting in the kitchen, a large pan of green beans beside her.

"They said tell you they were at the vacant lot, and they're going to dig for gold in that cave. You can catch'em if you hurry."

"It's too hot to hurry. Can I sit here with you instead?"

"Set right down and take a load off your feet."

Mrs. Wacker picked up the beans but her hands didn't work with their usual speed. She snapped a bean into three parts and dropped them one by one into the kettle. Lou Emma took a handful, snapped them, and reached for more. The clock on the kitchen shelf ticked loudly.

"I'm sorry comp'ny," Mrs. Wacker apologized. "Every year I get a spell like this. I call it the Chautauqua Blues."

"The Chautauqua Blues?"

Mrs. Wacker dropped an unsnapped bean into the kettle. "Every year I think, *this* year I'll take the girls to Chautauqua. Rent a tent, buy season tickets, do it up brown. And every year something happens to keep me from it. Taxes, doctor bills, one time our horse, Ned, up'n' died. No matter what, it always happens."

"Yes ma'am," Lou Emma said solemnly, not knowing what else to say.

"A person'd think I'd stop planning, but I don't."

"No ma'am." Then Lou Emma ventured, "I'm sorry."

Mrs. Wacker blinked. "Land o' hope an' glory, child, don't feel sorry for me. I've got more blessings than a blackberry patch has chiggers. Are you folks going?"

"I don't know. Papa won't out'n' out say. That mostly means 'no.' "

"Well, don't pester him." Mrs. Wacker snapped beans with quick, efficient motions. "He's got a hard row to hoe. Let's plan for next year."

Lou Emma said, "I know a girl that made three dollars selling salve. Her mother bought half and gave it for Christmas presents."

"Good idea," Mrs. Wacker nodded. "I could clear out that room at the back and rent it to a college student. That is, if we knew one that didn't mind family."

"In *Little Women* Jo sold her hair," Lou Emma said.

"See there? Three ways a'ready. We'll both make it next year."

"I know I'm forgetting something," Professor Mil-

ler knocked his forehead with his knuckles as he stood
in the kitchen after breakfast.

"Is it H-O-G?" Lou Emma looked in his book bag
and found it, safe.

"Is it your Greek Lexicon? Eppie'n' me are using
it to press ferns," Maddy said. "Put fern seeds in your
shoes and you'll be invisible."

"Whatever this is it might as well be invisible," he
fretted, and drove off in the Great Smith.

At noon he still couldn't remember. "Did I mean
to order that new book of the Kansas poet who writes
as 'Ironquill'?"

"No, Papa," both girls assured him.

"Well, it may come to me. What are you two doing this afternoon?"

"Going blackberrying with Vinnie'n' Eppie," Lou
Emma said.

"Fine. Put sulphur in your shoes to keep off
chiggers."

"Were you trying to remember to say we could go
to Chautauqua?"

"Now, Maddy, I warned you . . . I don't see how
I can with all the work piled up. Work comes before
play." He went away and Maddy fumed.

"Maybe we can go next year," Lou Emma was putting away the silverware.

"I don't want to go next year. I want to go now.

Wait," Maddy took the silverware from Lou Emma
and dropped the pieces, one by one, into their slotted
spaces, chanting, "This year, next year, now, never.
This year, next year . . ." The last fork dropped as
never.

Lou Emma dived under the table and came up
with a spoon. "You dropped this and said you'd get
it when you swept. Only you didn't sweep."

"Hurrah!" Maddy dropped the unwashed spoon.
"*This year.* You see, I was right not to sweep." She
grabbed the broom and waltzed a couple of turns.

"Come on," Lou Emma said. "Here's the girls. Get
the berry buckets."

The road to the berry patch was long, hot, and
dusty. The first patch they found had been stripped.

"Tommy and his gang," Eppie said. "I saw'em
head out this way."

"Tommy sells berries and buys cigarettes," Vinnie
said.

"I don't b'lieve that about Tommy," Lou Emma
said.

"Hackberry told me. Tommy had a package of
cigarettes and he gave Hackberry the picture from it.
A lady in *tights.*"

Before such evidence, Lou Emma retreated. She
changed the subject. "Maddy, we forgot to put sulphur in our slippers for the chiggers."

"Aw, let the chiggers get their own sulphur," Maddy said crossly. "There's no more berries here. We came after berries."

"There's plenty in Owens' pasture," Vinnie insisted. "I said to go there in the first place, but she always has to be the big cheese."

There were, indeed, plenty of berries in Owens' pasture, well protected by a thicket of thorny canes. Soon the girls' arms and hands were criss-crossed with scratches. The berries were warm from the sun and bursting with juice. For every berry that went into the buckets, another went into their mouths. Tongues and lips were blue-black, dresses stained.

Eppie looked at the sun, low in the west. "We'd better go home."

"Mama'll make us take a salt bath to kill chiggers. We need a bath anyway so we won't care so much when she makes us," Vinnie said.

"Nobody makes us take baths," Maddy boasted. "Girls with mothers have always *got* to do this and *got* to do that. We do things when we want to."

"You'd better want to take a bath, or sleep with the pigs," Vinnie said.

"And stop talking against our Mama," Eppie said.

"Don't start to fuss," Lou Emma begged. "We've got too far to go."

For once Maddy listened to Lou Emma. The four started down the dusty road, swinging their full buckets. But the road home seemed twice as long as it had coming out. Lou Emma had a stone bruise on her heel that throbbed.

"How much further?" she asked Vinnie.

" 'Bout a hundred miles," Vinnie said gloomily. "We'll be late to supper an' Mama'll be madder'n a wet hen."

"Supper? *Ook!*" Lou Emma said, the blackberries in her stomach rebelling.

Then they heard the sound of wheels and hoofs. It was the shabby buggy and the wheezy mare that belonged to Miss Kate, but at the moment Lou Emma thought it looked like Cinderella's golden coach.

"Miss Kate . . ." she ran out into the road.

"Lou Emma? Maddy?" Miss Kate reined up in astonishment.

"We've been picking blackberries," Maddy explained.

"I'd never have guessed it," Miss Kate laughed. "May I offer you a ride home?"

"Yes, *ma'am,*" they all four chorused.

"Then put your berry buckets in the back and pile in."

With a comic look of resignation Hepzie, the mare, heaved her washboard sides and started down the road.

Chapter 8

The buggy stopped at the Millers' house. Hepzie's head drooped. The girls who had been chattering like blackbirds were suddenly quiet.

Hackberry shouted from the trapeze bar. "Where'd you go after blackberries? Topeka? You're goin' to catch it."

Around the corner of the grape arbor Mrs. Wacker advanced, carrying a sprinkler can. She set it down with a thump. "Where've you girls *been?*"

"Owens' pasture," Vinnie said in a small voice. "We brought you a whole lot of berries."

"More inside than out, from the way you look. I'm s'prised anybody'd pick up such a bunch of hard cases."

"This is Miss Kate Turner, our friend." Maddy introduced her with a proprietary air. "She's known us since the day we came to Gloriosa."

Mrs. Wacker bobbed her red head toward Miss Kate, but she wouldn't be cheated of the scolding she had been saving up for the girls. "It's less'n an hour till full dark, and you girls stravaging around in the woods. Don't you have a lick o' sense?"

Lou Emma didn't know whether to say they did or they didn't.

"Two buckets of berries," Eppie tried to placate her mother. "Real good ones. Miss Kate said so."

"You can have mine, too," Lou Emma said not caring if she never ate another blackberry till she was ninety-nine years old.

"I s'pose I ought to be thankful to get you back, though I don't exactly know why," Mrs. Wacker grumbled. "Won't you come in, Miss Kate? I declare these girls have me so r'iled up I forgot my manners."

"No thanks, I'm going back to the shop. I've been out looking for a room to rent, but with the college term starting they're very scarce."

"Hello, everybody." It was Professor Miller, carrying a book, his finger marking the page he had been reading. That meant he hadn't missed the girls. There would be no scolding, but Lou Emma was conscious of a little pang. It was kind of *cozy* to be scolded, only not too much.

"Miss Turner?" he held out his hand. "How nice to see you again."

"I'm glad to see you again, Professor. I got to Gloriosa by your directions."

"The girls told me about your millinery shop. You made a big impression on them as to the importance of appearance." A sick, stricken look came over his face. "Appearance. Appearance. Great Caesar's ghost!"

"Papa! Papa!" Lou Emma and Maddy jumped from the buggy.

"Are you sick, Professor?" Mrs. Wacker said.

"Yes. No. I don't know," he said distractedly.

"Is there anything I can do?" Miss Kate asked.

"Nothing, nothing at all." Professor Miller ran his hand through his hair. "When I spoke about 'appearance' I suddenly recalled what I had been trying to think of all day long."

"What is it?" Lou Emma clutched his arm.

"Tell us," Maddy jumped with impatience. "Is it something awful?"

"It's not awful, and it has nothing to do with the teaching of History, which is what I am employed by the college to do. I have been outlining an important chapter in Gibbon, very important, and . . ."

"Tell us what you're talking about or I'll drop dead," Maddy stormed. "Right here in the street. And Lou Emma'll drop dead with me."

"All right, Maddy, calm down." Professor Miller inhaled. "Dr. and Mrs. Biddle are entertaining the faculty and trustees of the college this evening. Mrs. Biddle asked that I come and that you girls 'put in an appearance.' "

Into the astounded silence that greeted his words, Hepzie turned her head and nickered inquiringly. Lou Emma looked at Maddy, and then at herself. Mud, dust, blackberry stain. Blood from a gash on a barbed wire fence.

"It's after seven," Professor Miller said. "The reception and musicale is at eight. We'd better forget it."

"If you would care to go alone," Miss Kate said, "the girls may come to the shop with me."

"No thank you. It was my fault. I should have remembered."

"I could've worn my pink tattefa," Maddy wailed. "I mean taffeta."

"Mrs. Biddle'll never forgive us," Lou Emma said.

"Oh, it can't be that serious. I'll speak to her tomorrow. This chapter in Gibbon deals with the idea of . . ."

"Hold on, Professor," Mrs. Wacker said. "I don't

know your friend Gibbon, but I do know Lavinia Biddle. If you don't show up tonight there's likely not to *be* any tomorrow."

"It's only a social occasion," Professor Miller said.

"Ex-actly," Mrs. Wacker said. "Go ahead. Leave the girls to me."

Professor Miller stiffened. "I don't think you understand, Mrs. Wacker. Rule Number One in our family is . . ."

"I know about your Rules, Professor, but I know Lavinia, and . . ."

"We can get the girls ready for the party if we all turn in instead of standing here talking," Miss Kate said. She wrapped the reins around the buggy whip and got out.

"I can't permit you to take your evening," Professor Miller said, "to correct what was my fault. I'll take the consequences."

"Fiddle-faddle," Miss Kate laughed. "Who cares whose fault? Do you girls want to go?"

"Yes, yes, double-dyed yes," they squealed happily.

"Then we'll get you ready. This will be a lot more fun than stitching ribbon at the shop all evening. Are your dresses in the top tray of your trunk upstairs?" Miss Kate started for the house before Lou Emma could get over her knowing where the Miller girls kept their best things.

"That's the way I like a person, with git-up-an'-git," Mrs. Wacker said. "Eppie'n' Vinnie, start water to heatin' in Millers' kitchen. Professor, get out your glad rags."

"I have the evening clothes I got to wear at my class reunion at Yale. Do you really think . . ."

"I really think," Mrs. Wacker said. "Come here, Lou Emma. I'll get the first layer of dirt off you out here. Peel off those stockings."

She took the sprinkler can and poured water down Lou Emma's bare legs. It was cold, cold, cold as ice. "Back, now front, now back again."

The gash on Lou Emma's arm from the barbed wire was opened again by the washing. Mrs. Wacker shook her head. "Hackberry, bring me some turpentine."

The turpentine stopped the bleeding, but oh, how it smelled! Lou Emma trotted into the kitchen smelling like a newly painted house. Miss Kate was hustling around as if she had lived there for years. She had the ironing board set up on the backs of two chairs, and she slipped the blue taffeta on it.

"You're lucky to be a blue-eyed blonde," she told Lou Emma.

"Mrs. Doctor Waters in Auden said we'd be pretty if we had . . . somebody . . . to look after us."

Miss Kate gave a little snort and spit on her finger

to test the heat of the iron. "You're pretty on your own. But what's that smell?"

"Turpentine." She explained about the gash from the fence.

"Whew! We'll have to do something about that. Go up and start taking a bowl bath, and hurry."

In the bedroom Lou Emma splashed water into the china washbowl. Maddy arrived and splashed in more water. They scrubbed with wash cloths, passing the soap back and forth. The water turned a grubby gray.

Miss Kate came in with the freshly ironed dresses over her arm. She took a hair brush to Lou Emma's hair so hard that with every stroke Lou Emma's head jerked back. "I think you've got a sand-burr in there. Pretty hair. Wish we had time to put it up on kid curlers."

Mrs. Wacker came into the little room, too, and brushed on Maddy's hair. Vinnie and Eppie found spots to sit on the bed.

"My tie? Where's my white tie?" Professor Miller bellowed from below.

"Look in the chifferobe," Lou Emma called back.

"*Tempus* is *fugitting*," he added. Miss Kate looked at the watch pinned to her dress.

"They'll be ready before you are," she challenged him.

"We'll never make it," Mrs. Wacker despaired. "Stand still, Maddy."

"Yes we will," Miss Kate snapped. "Stand still, Lou Emma."

"Where's my sash? My pink taffeta sash?" Maddy wailed. "I can't go without my sash. It's back in Auden. I remember I left it at Ella Johnson's when we played Flying Dutchman at her birthday party." She flung herself on the bed, wailing, "I can't go, I can't go, I c-c-c-can't."

"Yes you can." Miss Kate reached out the hairbrush and gave Maddy a sharp rap. "Get up from there. We'll think of something."

Startled, Maddy got up without another word.

"I've got a pink sash on my dotted Swiss," Eppie said. "There's some jelly on it at one end. Grape jelly."

"Go get it," Mrs. Wacker commanded, and Eppie and Vinnie scooted out.

"Get some cornstarch to dust on those scratches on your arms," Miss Kate told Lou Emma. "It covers better than talcum."

Scuffling through the things in the kitchen safe, Lou Emma found the cornstarch. She stole a moment to press her cheeks against the metal door.

It would be like this if we had somebody that belonged to us.

Hackberry came to the side door and thrust a frosted glass bottle in at Lou Emma. "Here. *She* told me to go to her shop'n' get it. I'll bet that Hepzie never went so fast since she was broke to harness." He departed.

Almost fearfully Lou Emma took out the ornamental glass stopper. The sweet familiar scent of roses floated out. She fairly flew upstairs.

"Cologne," Miss Kate dabbed the cool liquid on Lou Emma's neck, arms, and behind her ears, "to kill the turpentine smell."

Now, softly, silkily, the taffeta dresses, still warm from the iron, slipped over their heads. Miss Kate buttoned Lou Emma's back; Mrs. Wacker buttoned Maddy's back. Miss Kate took Eppie's sash and cut off the jelly stain. "I'll give you a new one tomorrow, Eppie. There's one at the shop."

"Stockings and slippers," Mrs. Wacker said. "Hurry."

As Lou Emma put on her slippers she felt the lucky penny under her heel. *Wish I might, wish I may, get the wish I wish today.*

The Biddle house was on Eclectic Avenue, a big brick house with wide porches. From every window electric lights twinkled. Gloriosa had had electric power since 1900, but most private homes were still

lighted with kerosene lamps or the Kansas-made
Coleman gasoline lanterns. Electric lights in a home
were a mark of leadership. Also, they meant that a
party must end by eleven P.M. as the power was
turned off at that time.

People were hurrying to the party. The light summer dresses the ladies wore fluttered against the nas-
turtiums bordering the walk.

"Professor Miller, how nice to see you. And the
girls."

It was Mrs. Advanced Mathematics Crawford. Lou
Emma smiled sweetly but stuck out her tongue behind Mrs. Crawford's back. Faculty wives tacked on
"and the girls" as an afterthought. Just one time she
would like to hear one say, "How nice to see you
girls. And your father."

"I'll bet our mother was prettier'n Mrs. Crawford,"
she said to Maddy.

"Prettier'n Miss Kate?"

Lou Emma hesitated, then said firmly, "Lots prettier."

The Biddles' front parlor was decorated with Bos-
ton ferns and baskets of tiger lilies. Rows of spindly
gilt chairs were arranged in front of the big grand
piano. Green velvet portieres divided the front parlor from the dining room. The velvet trembled and
Tommy looked out from the folds. He winked, and

jerked his thumb over his shoulder in the sign for "Come on."

"Let's skedaddle," Maddy said.

It was too late. Mrs. Biddle called to them to come over to the receiving line. She was elegantly dressed, and she looked as if she wouldn't even recognize a wet mop if she saw one. Her dress was changeable lavender silk, draped across the bosom with a tracery of shiny beads. Above her pompadoured hair quivered a jeweled aigrette.

"So glad you could come." She gave the girls a firm handshake and sent them down the line. There was no possible escape.

One by one Lou Emma took the outstretched hands, murmuring that she was Professor Miller's daughter . . . ha-ha . . . and very glad to be here. The names of those in the receiving line slid in and out of her ears. Only the last one stuck. Mr. Garrett.

"Quick, skiddoo," Maddy said, in a loud whisper.

"Madeline Margaret and Louisa Emmaline," Mrs. Biddle said sweetly. "I want you especially to hear the musicale. Your chairs are in the front row."

Lou Emma surprised a twinkle in the eyes of the lean, brown-faced man she had just met. Had Mr. Garrett heard Maddy's whisper? Solemnly, the Miller girls sat down in the front row. Mrs. Biddle hurried late-comers down the line, then she struck a chord on the piano. They would be favored, she announced, by musical numbers by the Fine Arts faculty.

Miss Claudel played the violin. Miss Lawrence played the piano. Mr. Meagher sang. Then Mrs. Meagher sang. Then Miss Claudel and Miss Lawrence were joined by other instrumentalists.

The gilt chairs became instruments of torture. They creaked at every motion. Lou Emma's sash bow-knot dug into her back. All around the Miller girls, grownup faces were polite and smiling, grownup hands applauded the endless music. The fans the ladies carried moved in gentle rhythms. Only the Miller girls squirmed and twisted; only their chairs creaked.

How will we ever learn to be grownup?

A male quartet sang: "The bells in the lighthouse ring, ding dong . . ."

"I itch," Maddy whispered.

"Ding *dong,* the bells in the lighthouse ring . . ."

"I itch something awful."

As if Maddy had called a plague down on her, Lou Emma began to itch. Back of her knees, around her waist, under her arms. Chiggers.

"I've got to scratch," Maddy said desperately.

"Not now. Mrs. Biddle's watching us."

"And the bells in the lighthouse ring . . . *ding dong.*"

The quartet bowed. The grownups applauded. The quartet started an encore.

"Many brave hearts are asleep in the deep . . . so be-ware, be-ware."

Creak-creak, Maddy's chair creaked as she scratched. Ladies near stopped fanning to watch. Itching that was pure agony hit Lou Emma. She scratched with her sister.

"Be-ware," thundered the bass. "Beware . . ."

Lou Emma signaled Maddy and they rose and tip-toed from the front parlor out through the French doors to the side porch, scratching as they went. Behind them the bass singer boomed, *"Bee-ware, Bee-ware . . ."*

"Ahhh!" the Miller girls sighed in relief, scratching steadily. The night breeze fanned them. They held the taffeta of their dresses away from their backs where it had sweated to them and felt the delicious cool. The first wave of itching diminished.

Cigar smoke drifted past. A man chuckled. "You been blackberrying?"

"How'd you guess?" Lou Emma said, as Maddy got in a few more digs behind her.

"I watched you through the door. Blackberries and chiggers go together."

"Papa told us to put sulphur in our shoes," Maddy said. "We forgot."

" 'Twouldn't have made a nickel's worth of difference. Your real, dyed-in-the-wool Kansas chigger thrives on sulphur."

"Mrs. Wacker says take salt baths," Maddy said.

"Jane knows better'n that. Salt baths just keep you busy so you won't notice the itching. You rub those bites with salt pork when you get home."

"Ugh!" they gagged.

The man chuckled and his cigar glowed bright.

"Why, you're Mr. Garrett," Lou Emma said. "We met you in the line."

"That's right. It happens I like my music outdoors."

They listened happily as the quartet sang *Annie Laurie.*

"I asked for that," Mr. Garrett said. "My mother came from Scotland."

Through the crack in the French doors they heard Mrs. Biddle say she had prevailed on Professor Mowrer to give some oratorical selections.

"Oh-oh," Mr. Garrett said. "We're in for it now."

"Wonder where Tommy went?" Maddy said.

"The Biddle boy?" Mr. Garrett's cigar pointed. "Climb the porch railing and go 'round back. I'll lay even money he's hanging around the refreshments."

"One-two-three, jump." They landed in the soft dirt of a flower bed.

"He's nice," Maddy said. "Who is he anyway?"

"The man that gave the land for the college," Lou Emma unsnagged her skirt from a climbing rose. "The man we chased the cows of."

They dodged under the windows of the house to avoid being seen. Tommy sat hunched on the back steps. "You were long enough gettin' here," he said grumpily.

"What's that out there?" Maddy pointed to a dim white form visible against the blackness of the barn. "Looks like a ghost." A chain rattled.

"Ghost nothin', that's my goat, Swish, that I told you about. I've got to keep'im on a chain because our hired girl, Hilda, says she'll quit if he butts her one more time. Hilda makes the best cake in town, and

Ma'll turn me wrongside out and swaller me whole if old Hilda quits."

Maddy looked in at the kitchen door. "Is that Hilda?"

"Yep. She's watchin' those cakes like they were solid gold."

The big-boned German girl sat by the kitchen table fanning herself with a folded newspaper. Four cakes were ranged in front of her. Tall, noble cakes with peaks of white icing. Lou Emma remembered they had had nothing for supper. Nothing but blackberries since noon.

"What else's for refreshments?" she asked.

"Ice cream." Tommy showed them the two big wooden freezers standing in tubs on the back porch. Each was covered by a gunny sack to keep the ice from melting. He lifted a sack. "Let's snitch some."

"Tommy," Hilda called, "stay out of the ice. If that cream don't hold your Ma'll be fit to be tied."

"Allllll right." Tommy dragged it out as he scratched loose chips from the top and put them into Maddy's and Lou Emma's mouths. They sat on the steps sucking the salty ice. "Want to see Swish? I'll bring him up."

Presently Tommy reappeared carrying a lantern and holding a light chain. At the end of the chain tripped a small white goat with horns just beginning to show and a beard just beginning to curl. In the lantern light his yellow eyes were bright and knowing, as if he had been born wise.

"Na-a-a-a-a," he walked up the slack of the chain to Lou Emma.

She put out her hand, cautiously, ready to jerk it back, and touched his head. Swish twitched his short stubby tail and pressed against her.

"I like him," Lou Emma said, amazed that she did. "He's cute."

"Where'd you get him?" Maddy rubbed the little goat between the horns.

"Traded up. Had a jackknife to start. Traded for a baseball bat. Traded for a mushrat trap. Caught some mushrats, skun 'em and sold the hides. Took the money and bought a talkin' machine motor off Gunny Gallagher. Traded the motor for a pound of taffy and a len'th of stovepipe with an elbow. Ate the taffy and it pulled my loose tooth. Traded the pipe and the tooth for a sled. Used the sled till the snow quit, then I found this kid that's folks were movin' to Iowa and traded the sled for Swish."

"I think that's wonderful," Lou Emma said and Tommy beamed.

"Hah! You could've got Swish for nothing," Maddy said. "When we moved to Kansas we gave away a million things free. Even our Maltese cat."

"A goat's more valuable than a cat," Lou Emma said to her sister.

"I'll say," Tommy agreed. "Ever see a cat stand on a rolling barrel? Well, Swish can. He's better'n Barnum an' Bailey on anything that rolls."

"Let's take him on the back step with us," Maddy said.

"Uh-uh. Not with Hilda in the kitchen," Tommy said. "She told my folks they oughta take Swish *to the slaughterhouse.*"

"Why, that's terrible," Lou Emma said.

"Na-a-a-a," Swish nudged her. "Nananana."

"Let's us go back," Maddy said. "She might cut the cake early."

Tommy looped the chain loosely over the fence and started for the kitchen with the girls. Haunted by the terrible word, *slaughterhouse,* Lou Emma thought he should put Swish in the barn.

"Aw, he's all right. He likes to be outdoors in good weather."

Hilda stopped fanning as they came into the kitchen, but held the newspaper poised. "Where's that *dumkopf* goat?"

Tommy rolled his eyes. "You know I promised, I took a Bible oath . . ."

"Shame to speak the word 'Bible' with that wicked goat around."

Lou Emma admired the cakes. "Wish I could make icing like that."

Hilda became interested. "You the girls from Ohio that keep house for your Pop? Come over one day, I'll show you how to make icing."

Applause sounded from the front parlor. Hilda glanced at the clock and cut three big slices of cake, put them on a plate and gave them to Lou Emma. "No need for them in there to have it all."

"Good old Hilda," Tommy said. "She's my chum."

She swatted at him with the paper. "Don't let that *dumkopf* goat have none of my cake."

They ran around to the side porch and climbed the railing. Mr. Garrett had gone. Sitting on the porch floor they ate the cake and watched the grown-ups inside. Maddy said it was like watching a fish-bowl where the fish swam up to each other, waved their fins, goggled their eyes, and swam away. But as they laughed at that until they choked on cake, a crash came from the back of the house.

It was followed by another. A rolling, thumping racket sounded. Bumpety-*bump,* bumpety-*bump. Bump, bump,* BUMP! A last thundering crash, then the clatter of sharp hoofs on steps.

"Swish! He slipped his chain." Tommy vaulted the railing and ran. Lou Emma and Maddy followed as fast as they could.

But when they reached the back yard he was not in sight. Dr. and Mrs. Biddle were there, and Swish, balancing on top of a rolling ice-cream freezer. The second freezer rolled into the darkness, ice and water pouring on the ground. Swish deftly reversed his feet, bobbed his head, and bleated as the top bounced from the rolling freezer can. Ice glittered in the yard.

The Miller girls hid in the shadows. Lou Emma's heart was pounding.

"Thomas Biddle," his mother's tone was ominous. "Come here."

"He ran the steps under," Hilda called shrilly.

"Tommy, step out here, right now." Dr. Biddle said. No answer came.

"Na-a-a-a," Swish bleated, and leaped from the rolling freezer and galloped off into the darkness. Only then did Tommy come from his hiding place. Angry voices filled the back yard.

". . . told you a thousand times if I've told you once."

". . . keep him chained. You promised."

". . . your Bible oath you took. Take shame to yourself."

". . . salt in the ice-cream. It won't be fit to eat."

Then the word Lou Emma had been fearing. "Slaughterhouse." And again, louder, beyond mistake, *"Slaughterhouse!"*

Chapter 9

There wasn't a sound in the room, nor a sound in the world outside. Moonlight filtered through elm leaves dappled the floor around the window. What had waked Lou Emma? She didn't know. She only knew something had.

The moonlight made the corners of the room dark and scary. Was it there? No, whatever it was, it was outside the house.

Plip . . . plip-plip.

That was what had waked her. But what was it?

Lou Emma sat up in bed, one hand touching Maddy's back for courage. Then on the floor in a puddle of moonlight she saw some pebbles. A shower of them rattled in at the open window.

In a moment, kneeling at the low window-sill, looking down through the whispering leaves she saw Tommy. Beside him was Swish, ghostly white.

"Tommy," she called softly. "It's me, Lou Emma."

"Come down," he called back hoarsely.

She rummaged in a drawer for her challis dressing gown, and barefoot, to keep from making a sound, she came down the steps. Holding her breath, she passed her father's room but he did not wake. She padded through the dark, stuffy kitchen, unlatched the side door, and stepped outside.

Tommy and Swish came over, soundless on the grass. Could this be happening, she wondered, or was she dreaming?

"What's the matter?"

"It's Swish," Tommy said, and choked. "I'm here because of Sw-Swish."

Why, he's been crying.

Tommy rubbed his nose with the back of his hand. Swish began to lick at Lou Emma's ankles. He must like the taste of the salt pork she had rubbed on at Mr. Garrett's direction.

"Ma says if she ever sees hide or hair of Swish again she'll take him to the slaughterhouse herself."

"Oh no," Lou Emma gasped.

"She says he's in-cor-rig-i-ble. But he's only a goat." Words tumbled from Tommy. "How'd a goat know there was ice-cream in those old freezers. He only liked to roll 'em around. He didn't mean to ruin the ice-cream."

Lou Emma bent over Swish and rubbed his hard little head. She could see his bright, watchful eyes. He was so alive; she couldn't bear for him not to be alive.

"Could you hide Swish? Keep him out of Ma's sight? Maybe she'd give in then, and let me keep him. Will you, Lou Emma?"

She didn't stop to think where she would keep a goat out of Mrs. Biddle's sight, or what her father might say, or anything. She put her hand out and took the chain, warm from Tommy's grasp.

"I'll keep him. Maddy'll help. We'll do it, somehow."

There was an awful moment when she thought Tommy was going to cry again. But he didn't. He put his hand over her hand that held Swish's chain.

"I'll never forget this, Lou Emma. You're the nicest girl I know."

"Na-a-a-a," Swish said. Tommy grabbed Swish's nose and clamped his mouth shut. The goat struggled and pulled them under the grape arbor before he became quiet.

"But he won't keep quiet forever," Lou Emma said. The problems of keeping a goat hidden were

beginning to rise up before her. Resolutely she pushed them down. Swish needed help and Tommy had asked her and she had promised. All she needed to do to stiffen her courage was to think of the terrible word, *slaughterhouse.*

"I'll put him in the barn," Tommy said. "And tomorrow I'll bring his feed over."

"I thought goats ate tin cans."

"That's silly. They'll browse around stuff, but they're real finicky what they eat. Like Pa's shirt. Swish only ate that account of the starch. If old Hilda'd given him a dish of starch, but not her." Tommy hesitated. "There's one more thing."

"What is it?"

"Aw, it's nothin' bad. Swish dearly loves cigarettes."

As if he understood the word, Swish rattled his chain.

"You mean he smokes?" Lou Emma was shocked in spite of herself.

"Naw, he eats 'em. I gathered snipes for him till Ma saw me in front of the Pool Hall, and gave me what-for. After that I picked berries to sell and bought Swish his own cigarettes."

"Oh, Tommy, I said you didn't smoke. Hackberry told Vinnie . . ."

"That little wart."

"You mustn't smoke," she said earnestly. "My Aunt Jesse says cigarettes are coffin nails. One drop of nicotine on the tongue of a dog . . ."

"I know. Ma jaws me all the time. But I buy'em for Swish is all. Punk Williams gets'em for me. The low-down cuss is eighteen and can buy'em himself and he charges me twice the store price. Here." He put a package in her hand.

Should she drop it to the ground and grind it under her heel? Carry Nation would. But Tommy was in enough trouble, she mustn't make him feel worse. Sniffing the tobacco, Swish nuzzled her hand. She fed him a cigarette and he gave a joyous jump. It didn't seem to hurt him a bit.

A clock in the distance struck one solemn note. The Millers' clock echoed it from the kitchen. It seemed much later than it had before.

"You go on in," Tommy said. "I'll put Swish in the barn."

She almost offered to go with him, then it came to her that he wanted to be alone to say goodbye to his pet.

"Good night," she whispered and ran soft-footed into the kitchen. Upstairs, kneeling by the window-sill, she waited.

Presently the solitary figure of Tommy Biddle came from the direction of the barn. Head down, he

plodded through the yard to the silent street. Lou
Emma watched him until he was out of sight.

The next morning she slept late and when she
waked Maddy was gone. A smell of bacon and coffee
came from the kitchen. *S'pose they've found Swish.*
Lou Emma hurried downstairs.

"Why didn't you call me?" she asked her father
and Maddy.

"I decided you needed your beauty sleep after the
party," Professor Miller said. "Maddy was down when
I came in to make the coffee, so we let you sleep."

"I got up to rub more salt pork on my chigger
bites," Maddy said. "Tell me some more about Kansas and the Underground Railroad, Papa."

"Well, I told you girls before we moved here that
this was Bleeding Kansas, that the War began earlier
and lasted longer here than any place else. Kansas
and Missouri . . ." And he was off on stories of the
Border Wars.

Lou Emma sugared her oatmeal, her face down.
She was sure that S-W-I-S-H was written in fiery
letters across her forehead. If only she had waked
early and asked Maddy to help her. She must tell her
father about Swish before he went out to get the
Great Smith. But how . . . how . . . eating her
oatmeal in small bites, she began to realize that

Maddy was asking her father questions about the Civil War which she certainly knew the answers to. What was she doing?

"And that was how Quantrill burned Lawrence, Kansas," Professor Miller said. He sliced some bread and put it in the four-sided toaster that stood on the kitchen range.

"Why'd Quantrill do it?" Maddy asked.

"There are many reasons to be considered," Professor Miller said in his classroom voice. "First . . ."

"The toast, Papa, the toast."

Black smoke came from the toaster. Professor Miller dropped the ruined slices into the range and sliced more bread. "As I was saying . . ."

"Na-a-a-a-a." Faint but unmistakable came the sound.

Professor Miller looked up. "What's that?"

Lou Emma hastily filled her mouth with oatmeal.

"Na-a-a-a-a."

"What did you start to say 'In the first place?' " Maddy asked.

"The reasons behind such an action . . ." Professor Miller looked from one girl to the other. "Why this sudden interest in history, young ladies?"

"We love to hear you talk, Papa," Maddy said.

"You can tell History better'n our school books," Lou Emma said.

"Na-a-a-a." Then again, louder. "Na-a-a-a."

"That's the Biddle boy's goat." He looked at the girls. "Isn't it?"

The clock ticked louder and louder.

"I said, 'Isn't it?'"

"Yessir," Lou Emma said, all her chigger bites starting to itch.

"What is it doing here?"

"Eating oatmeal," Maddy said. "Raw, not cooked. I was going to tell you he was here, Papa, only we got to talking . . . about . . . the . . . Civil . . . War."

"Lou Emma? Speak now or forever hold your peace."

"Well. Tommy brought him here last night. He threw some stones in our window and I went down. Maddy was asleep. And Mrs. Biddle says if she sees him one more time she'll take him to the . . . the . . ." Lou Emma's voice was shaking like apple jelly. "And I promised, Papa, I promised."

"Promised what? Mrs. Biddle will take who, where?"

"Take Swish to the . . . slaughterhouse."

"No!" Maddy banged the table. The silverware jumped.

"I promised Tommy I'd keep Swish hid here," Lou Emma said.

"Are you stark raving crazy?" Professor Miller said. "Have you thought what will happen when Mrs. Biddle discovers the History Department is concealing a goat?"

"We can keep him out of her sight," Maddy said confidently.

"Tommy thinks she'll get over it and let him have Swish back."

"After that business with the ice-cream?" Professor Miller snorted. "That would try the patience of a saint, and Mrs. Biddle is not a saint."

"The ice-cream wasn't so very salty," Lou Emma said.

"It was salty as brine," Maddy said. "But Swish didn't mean any harm."

"Mrs. Murphy's cow didn't mean any harm kicking over the lantern, but Chicago burned just the same," Professor Miller said.

"It's Hilda that wants him to go to the slaughterhouse," Maddy said. "Because he butted her in the back. That's not turning the other cheek very much."

"Hilda calls him a *dumkopf* goat," Lou Emma said.

"I'd be a *dumkopf* parent if I let you keep that creature."

They began to weep. Maddy in loud sobs, Lou Emma in a steady wail.

The smell of burning toast filled the kitchen. Professor Miller jerked the toaster off the range. It hit the floor, blackened slices of bread scattered, smoking like burnt offerings. Trying to pick up the toaster Professor Miller burned his thumb, stuck it into his mouth, kicked the toaster, and glared at his daughters.

"*Sanguine Saturnini!*" He took his thumb from his mouth, shook it to cool it, and said between clenched teeth, "*SANGUINE SATURNINI!*"

This was their father's most terrible oath. They had never dared ask him what it meant, but they knew it was at the furthest limits of his patience. They stopped crying immediately. Professor Miller spread butter on his burned thumb.

"Now girls," he sat down at the table. This was his first-day-of-the-term manner. "We have a problem to solve, but not by tears or sentimentality."

"Yessir."

"We must proceed logically, striving for the greatest good for the greatest number. Is that agreed?"

They nodded solemnly.

"The logical way to approach a problem is through its various parts."

Lou Emma looked hopelessly at Maddy who was rolling bread pills. Swish was as good as on his way to the slaughterhouse.

"Therefore," Professor Miller concluded, "it is only logical that the goat, Swish, be returned to the Biddles. Agreed?"

"No!" Maddy said.

"No!" Lou Emma said.

"But you agreed to my arguments. In the interest of logic . . ."

"Tommy gave him to me and I promised." Panic was making Lou Emma's voice quiver again. "You've told us a million times to keep promises."

"I have also told you a half-million times not to make promises you cannot keep. Now, I will return the goat to the Biddles and we'll forget about it."

"No!" Lou Emma said.

"No!" Maddy said.

"Good morning."

The three Millers turned. Miss Kate was standing outside the door, smiling, a pink rosebud at the collar of her pink shirtwaist, a Leghorn hat shading her face. "I hope I'm not interrupting your break-fast."

"Not at all." Professor Miller recovered first. "Come in and have some coffee. We've just been discussing . . . logic."

"Thank you, but I only came by for my handbag. I left it last night."

"Ask *her* about Swish," Lou Emma burst out.

"Swish?" Miss Kate asked.

"A dear little darling little goat, and Papa's going to murder him," Maddy said.

"Really?" Miss Kate's dark eyes widened.

"Not all by himself," Lou Emma felt bound to explain. "But he's going to let it happen if he makes us give Swish back to the Biddles."

"Miss Turner doesn't want to hear all this," Professor Miller said.

Miss Kate's foot tapped. "Will you please stop deciding for me what I want to do? I want to hear about Swish. And my name is Kate."

"Very well, Kate. To get to the goat we must first . . ."

"Perhaps I had better have that coffee, after all." Miss Kate came in and sat at the table. Maddy poured her a cup of coffee.

All three of the Millers, each interrupting the other, told the story.

"That's that," Professor Miller said at last. "What's your verdict?"

Miss Kate fingered the rosebud at her collar. "I haven't heard the accused, himself. Where's Swish?"

"Wait on the side steps. We'll bring him," Maddy said.

They ran for the barn. Maddy beat Lou Emma, who looked back over her shoulder at her father and

Miss Kate sitting on the steps. Those steps were too narrow for grownups to be very far apart.

Swish greeted them with loud complaints. His chain was tangled. He had upset his waterbucket, and knocked the oatmeal into the dirt.

"We've got to clean him up. Miss Kate thinks first impressions are important," Lou Emma said.

Lou Emma brushed one side, Maddy the other. Laughter came from the steps. Lou Emma peeked through the barn door. "Miss Kate's got the rosebud off her collar and given it to Papa. He's sniffing it."

"Silly as silly as silly." Maddy brushed on Swish.

Professor Miller put the rosebud into the lapel of his coat, but Lou Emma didn't mention it, fearing Maddy's remarks.

"Oh, Lou Emma, if Papa won't let us keep Swish, I can't stand it."

"Me neither. Do you think Miss Kate can get him to?"

"What can she do?" Maddy mourned. "Aunt Jesse couldn't make Papa do anything, and she was his only sister."

"Miss Kate got him to take us to Biddle's party."

"That's right," Maddy admitted. "Do you think . . ."

Suddenly, Lou Emma was afraid of Maddy's question. "Let's go ahead now. Swish is getting fidgety."

The little white goat seemed to know exactly what they wanted him to do. He trotted up to the steps and stood in front of Miss Kate and Professor Miller, his golden eyes bright and unafraid, his tail twitching merrily.

"Na-a-a-a-a," he said.

"Look at his little horns," Lou Emma said.

"And his little beard," Maddy said.

"I don't see a goat," Professor Miller said. "I see Trouble with a capital T. Surely you understand that, Kate."

"Oh I understand. And I quite agree with you."

Lou Emma's heart did a flip-flop.

"It's ridiculous to discuss," Professor Miller said.

"Preposterous," Miss Kate nodded. "You're absolutely right."

"Why are we wasting time talking about it?"

"I can see that it's out of the question," Miss Kate said.

"Foolish. Sentimental." Professor Miller absently scratched Swish's back.

"How well you put it," Miss Kate said. "How logically."

The ground was dropping away under Lou Emma's feet. Maddy stood, gulping, fists clenching and unclenching. They had failed Swish, and Miss Kate had failed them.

"On the other hand," Professor Miller said. "There are circumstances . . ."

"The whole thing is illogical," Miss Kate said.

"Look here," Professor Miller said, "logic isn't everything in life."

"I can return Swish to the Biddles for you," Miss Kate said. "I'm going out that way this morning to deliver a special order."

Lou Emma saw her father move uncomfortably on the steps. He crossed and uncrossed his long legs.

"I wouldn't think of putting you to the trouble," he replied stiffly.

"No trouble at all. The girls can hobble his back legs, and . . ."

"No," Maddy put her fingers in her ears and went on saying, "No . . . no . . ."

Lou Emma stared at Miss Kate, horrified. Then she caught the flicker of a brown eyelash. What was she up to?

"I'm going right past the Biddles' home."

"No." Professor Miller said. "No, we're keeping Swish."

"Papa!" Lou Emma flung herself at him. Maddy went into a dance.

Miss Kate sat quietly smiling down at the step.

When the hullabaloo subsided Professor Miller looked at her. "How did it happen, Kate?"

"Oh Professor . . ." He held up his hand and and stopped her.

"If I call you Kate, it's only logical for you to call me Cyrus."

She shook her head. "You're the one who believes in logic, Professor. I believe in goats and girls. It was the girls who did it."

"Oh, Papa, I'm so glad," Lou Emma said contentedly.

"I knew you'd let us keep him, all the time," Maddy said.

"Then you knew more than I did." Professor Miller patted Swish's sleek hide. "Welcome to the family, *Capricornus*."

"Nanananan," Swish answered and neatly nipped off the rosebud in his lapel.

"Why, you miserable, cross-grained, bearded sinner!" Professor Miller half rose from the steps.

"No, Papa, you've welcomed him to the family," Lou Emma said.

"Rule Number One," Maddy said.

"I'll bring you another rosebud," Miss Kate laughed. "By the way, we'll be neighbors. Mrs. Wacker is renting me a room."

It seemed to Lou Emma that the world had turned to glittering beauty, the way it did when she looked through Vinnie's prism.

Chapter 10

Swish was more fun than any pet the Miller girls ever owned. They spent hours brushing his white coat, polishing his hoofs with shoe-blacking, and dressing him in un-goatlike costumes.

The Hopscotch game, the cave, the playhouse were deserted. The center of fun shifted to the Millers' yard. Vinnie, Eppie, and Hackberry were there every day. Mr. Wacker saved cigar butts for Swish. Mrs. Wacker made him a collar and hung a little bell on it. And of course Tommy came, and Tommy's gang.

"Everybody loves Swish," Lou Emma said as the Miller girls sat on top of the grape arbor with Swish staked out below them.

"Everybody but you-know-who." Maddy ate some

grapes and spit the seeds, trying to make each seed go farther than the last. "I'm s'prised she hasn't been nosing around. Mothers sure are nosy."

"Tommy says she's busy. He thinks she's forgot."

"Even Mrs. Wacker's nosy." Maddy warmed to her subject. "She wants to know every minute where Eppie an' Vinnie are *at,* who they're *with,* what they *said.*"

"Mothers have to be nosy or they'd never find out anything."

"Good gravy, Lou Emma, how'd you like to have to tell some old mother everything you do. Like why you were moonin' around with that picture you found at EKCC. 'President Amos T. Biddle and Wife and Son, Thomas.' "

"I was not moonin' around," Lou Emma said. "I was merely . . ."

"You were merely cutting Tommy's picture out and putting it under your pillow. I found it, and I'm going to tell Tommy."

"You wouldn't?" Lou Emma asked in agony. "You wouldn't?"

Maddy let her simmer a few minutes. "Nope. I wouldn't. But on account of Rule Number One. Not on account of you begging me."

"I don't care what it's on account of, as long as it is."

"I wish Miss Kate'd move in," Maddy spit seeds towards Wackers'.

"Mrs. Wacker wants the room painted and Mr. Wacker forgets to do it."

"Eppie says he's spent the paint money," Maddy said.

"Funny, how nice he can be, then . . . you know."

They sat quietly, eating grapes and spitting seeds at Swish.

Maddy, do you know what logic is?" Lou Emma asked.

"It's when Papa wants us to do something we don't

want to. He says we've got to because it's plain logic."

"I mean really. I asked Papa and he explained it for an hour and I'm not ever going to ask him again. But I don't know what it is. Do you?"

"It's like two and two make four." Maddy plucked four grapes and arranged them on a leaf. "Two here, two here. That's four, not five or three."

"If it's arithmetic, don't tell me." From her first day of school, arithmetic had been a thing Lou Emma feared and dreaded. A Dismal Swamp.

"Well, like this, then," Maddy said. "I ate green grapes; my stomach aches. See? When you do something, something happens because of what you did."

"Does it have to be arithmetic or stomach aches? Can't it be fun?"

"I don't think so." Maddy spit seeds like a seed-spitting machine. "Why do you want to know?"

"Papa thinks it's important. When he told Miss Kate, 'Logic isn't all there is to life,' he meant it was *nearly* all." Lou Emma lowered her voice. "How would you like to go to Chautauqua?"

"*Chautauqua?*" Maddy almost fell off the grape arbor. "But Papa said he could not take us. N-O-T. Dr. Biddle's run in Astronomy and Botany for him to teach, besides History, and he's worked ragged."

"I know all that," Lou Emma said. "I know he's working like a Trojan, even if I don't know why they worked so hard. But he could do better without having us underfoot."

"On top of the grape arbor's not underfoot," Maddy said crossly. "And he's got Rule Number Two: Never Interrupt Papa When He's Studying."

"Well, I've got a plan about Chautauqua," Lou Emma said, "only I don't know if it's logical or not."

"Let's walk down to Miss Kate's Chapeaux and you can tell me on the way." Maddy shinnied down the grape arbor. Lou Emma followed more slowly, stopping to pat Swish and assure him she would be back soon.

The Chautauqua banners were gay on Assembly Avenue, giving the town a carnival air. Each store window held some bargain offer connected with the coming event. It was impossible to live in Gloriosa and not be touched by Chautauqua.

Lou Emma explained her plan to Maddy. "Mrs. Wacker gave me the idea. She says she gets the Chautauqua Blues because she can't go and take the girls. Season tickets are a dollar'n' a half, and there's rent for the tent, and all. She said it'd be the last of a twenty-dollar goldpiece before it was done."

"What's that to do with us?"

"Well, remember last night when you threw out all the plants and stuff Papa'd collected for his class in Botany."

"It was a mistake. How was I to know . . ."

"Never mind. It got Papa pretty huffy. He was mad at me, too, because I spilt pancake batter on his Astronomy notes. He said I flooded the Big Dipper and wrecked a whole galaxy—whatever that is—and I wasn't ever to mix pancakes in the front room."

"I don't think that's Rule Number Three," Maddy said.

"Anyway, when you were putting Swish in the barn I dropped the wash-boiler and . . ."

"Was that what I heard? Swish nearly jumped out of his skin."

"So did Papa. He knocked over his ink bottle and spoilt a lot more notes, I don't know what about. He came stomping out to the kitchen and thumped the table and said he'd give a twenty-dollar goldpiece for some *peace, quiet, and order* around the place."

"I'll bet I can guess your plan," Maddy said, but Lou Emma shushed her. It was her plan and she was going to tell it herself.

"Mrs. Wacker doesn't have a twenty-dollar gold-piece, but Papa does. He keeps it in the box with his collar buttons, by our mother's picture."

"And he can give it to Mrs. Wacker and she can take us four girls to the Chautauqua and Papa can have the house to himself!" Maddy blurted out.

"Buttinski," Lou Emma complained. "But that's it to a T. What I want to know is, is it logical?"

"It's better'n logical," Maddy said. "It's fun."

"Then let's tell Miss Kate."

The millinery shop was a very different place from the one it had been the first time the Miller girls had seen it. Soap, water, paint, elbow grease, and good taste had turned the dreary little hole-in-the-wall into a pink and white bandbox. Gaily trimmed hats rested on tall hat stands. Two small dressing tables with large mirrors invited customers to try on hats. Pink curtains divided the sales room from the workroom where hats were created to order.

Gloriosa ladies had been quick to discover that Kate Turner could make a hat that was an ornament to any costume. Already her order book was filled for weeks ahead.

When the girls reached the shop one customer was trying on a black velvet with curled ostrich plumes, another admiring a white felt faced with blue watered silk. Miss Kate nodded for the girls to wait in the workroom. Lou Emma sat on the cot where Miss Kate slept. Maddy prowled among the rainbow of colors—bolts of ribbon, tulle, chiffon, bunches of bright flowers, bird wings, artificial fruit, hanks of gold and silver beads, myriads of spools of thread.

Miss Kate came in presently looking pleased. "Three hats sold today and more orders to get ready for Chautauqua. One for Mrs. Biddle, and she's always bought in Topeka. A dark green Gainsborough with amethyst satin ruching."

"We have a plan to go to Chautauqua," Maddy announced.

"It's my plan. I'll tell it." Lou Emma glared at her sister.

"Start right in," Miss Kate said, shaping pink velvet grapes on wire.

Hurriedly, to get ahead of Maddy's interruptions, Lou Emma recited her plan. "All we have to do is get Papa's and Mrs. Wacker's say-so."

"How about me?" Miss Kate lighted the gas plate to steam some ribbon. "I'm supposed to move into the Wackers' spare room sometime."

"Mr. Wacker hasn't bought the paint yet," Maddy said.

But a new and even more wonderful idea had come to Lou Emma. "Miss Kate! You come to the Chautauqua with us."

"You've got a cot," Maddy said. "All you have to do is shut up shop."

Miss Kate turned off the gas and faced the girls. "Would you really want me? Six in a tent is pretty crowded. Seven if you count Joy."

"Yes!" the girls shouted in concert. "Yes . . . yes . . . yes."

"Most of the stores in Gloriosa do close during Chautauqua," Miss Kate mused. "If I can get my orders out . . . and if Mrs. Wacker agrees . . . and your father, too . . . and if I can find time to make a hat for myself."

"Do you have to have a new hat?" Lou Emma said.

"It's good business for a milliner to wear new hats. Anyway, when I go out with my friends I always try to look my best."

"You always look pretty," Maddy said.

"No, I'm not pretty," Miss Kate said. "I'm neat, well-dressed, and well-pressed, and that's all. I had three pretty sisters and in Highbank I'm always known as 'the plain Turner sister.' "

The way I'm known as 'the good one,' Lou Emma understood. *And Miss Kate doesn't like it any better than I do.*

"So I decided to do the things the girls who were born pretty were too busy to do," Miss Kate said. "That's all there is to it."

"What kinds of things?" Maddy asked curiously.

"See here," Miss Kate said, "if we live seven in a tent you'll know my secrets soon enough. Run along and get Lou Emma's plan to working."

Running and walking by turns they got home and found Professor Miller in the kitchen, chipping ice to put into a glass of iced tea.

"*Quercus stellata,*" he muttered, pointing the ice pick at a heap of leaves on the table. "That's Post Oak. And *Toxylon pomiferum,* that's commonly known as Osage Orange, also as Hedge, also as Bowdark. Venus is the Evening Star sometimes and sometimes she isn't. Orion is south of the Gemini and has remarkable gaseous nebulae. Any more questions?"

"You're mixing up trees and stars," Maddy said.

"That's nothing to the way they're mixed up in my head." Professor Miller drank some iced tea. "If Dr. Biddle knew what I don't know about Astronomy . . ."

"We've come to help you, Papa," Maddy said.

Professor Miller looked alarmed. "The last time you helped me was by making laurel wreaths for the Roman history class. Only poison ivy got mixed in."

"You were the only one that broke out," Maddy reminded him.

"This is different," Lou Emma said. "This is a plan. And it's logical."

"My last effort at logic got me a goat, but I'll listen."

It was easy to tell the plan a third time. Lou Emma added a few new touches. "See how nice, Papa? Peace, quiet, and order for two weeks."

Her father pushed a chip of ice around the table top until Lou Emma couldn't stand his silence. "What's wrong? Isn't it logical?"

"It's logical all right. But I was only talking when I said that. I don't have a twenty-dollar goldpiece. The move out here, the Great Smith . . . I never should have bought it . . ."

"Oh yes you should," Maddy interrupted but he waved her to be quiet.

"And now Dr. Biddle says the college is in difficulties and we can't expect salaries until November. My dears, I don't have the money."

"But you do." Feeling like a heroine, having saved the best till last, Lou Emma brought the collar button box and handed the gold coin over.

"You'd forgotten, Papa," Maddy said. "You do have the money."

He fingered the little coin gently. "I guess I did forget . . . this."

"Then why in the world . . . " Maddy's question trailed into silence.

From the high point of a heroine, Lou Emma began to drop down, down.

"Your mother gave me this for a wedding gift. She said I was to save it until I found something I wanted more than gold."

Lou Emma was far down now. It was worse than when she had fallen from the cottonwood tree. Maddy stared mutely at the floor.

"I didn't know," Lou Emma whispered. "You never told us."

"Don't feel bad, girls." He pulled them over to him, one in the curve of each arm. "Your mother would never want you to be unhappy on her account. She was the happiest, laughingest person I ever knew. We laughed a lot over this very coin. I'd tell her I'd spent it for this or that, then I'd put it back in the box. Once I hid it a week and she nearly collapsed from curiosity."

"I'm sorry," Lou Emma said. "Put it back. It was a crazy plan."

"Yes," Maddy said. "Put it back where it was, Papa."

"It's a fine plan, and just what your mother would have wanted. I'd much rather have two weeks at Chautauqua for you two than a piece of gold."

"But you've saved it so long," Lou Emma said.

"You can save things too long. You can squeeze the very life out of things trying to hold onto them. It's high time this twenty-dollar goldpiece got back into circulation. Now, we'll go see what Mrs. Wacker says."

The screams of joy from the girls were so loud that Mrs. McKelvy said to Mr. McKelvy, "Those Miller girls! I don't see how the Professor puts up with 'em."

Chapter 11

At last they were at the Gloriosa Chautauqua Assembly. Lou Emma pinched herself and happily endured the throb of pain. It was real. For two weeks they would be tenters with the hundreds of others who had flocked in from all over the Middlewest.

From the front seat of the Great Smith Lou Emma looked out over acres of tents. They were arranged in rows along gravel-covered streets. Near their own tent, and many of the others she could see, was a coal-oil cookstove and a table for eating meals. Water faucets on the grounds already had puddles around them as tenters sloshed back and forth with buckets of water. Moss's ice wagon moved slowly along. She wondered if Tommy were on the back step, but probably he was helping his mother and Hilda at the Biddle tent.

The Miller-Wacker-Turner tent was near the slow-moving river. The manager warned them that they might find occasional toads in their tent, and that he could do nothing about the noise from the clanking rowboats for rent nearby. Pooh! Lou Emma would have slept *in* a rowboat *with* toads to get to come.

Heat rested on the grounds like a heavy blanket. The day was what Kansans called "a shirt sticker." Mrs. Wacker, unloading pots and pans, stopped often to mop her face with her apron. In the tent where Professor Miller was setting up the rented cots, his collar was wilted, his fair hair dark with sweat.

I'm going to have the cot next to Miss Kate if I have to . . .

Lou Emma paused to consider the things she would do to get that honored spot. Then she gave up and wriggled with impatience that Miss Kate had insisted on working this last day to get her orders out. She planned to come out tonight on the streetcar with her suitcase.

Lou Emma slid across the hot leather seat to a new patch of shade. Beside the tents she could see many of the permanent buildings of the Chautauqua. Normal Hall, Hall of Philosophy, Willard Hall, Hall of Religion. And she knew where the Dining Hall was where meals could be had for twenty-five cents. But even her limited arithmetic told her such extravagance would cause their twenty-dollar goldpiece to melt like ice in the sun. They would do their own cooking with food brought from home.

In the middle of the sprawling grounds was the mammoth Assembly Hall. It had a back and a front, but the sides were open. The big platform could accommodate an entire orchestra or the great chorus trained yearly at the Chautauqua. Here, every afternoon and night a special program would be presented, open to holders of season tickets. Single admissions were sold, too, but the season ticket holders felt that their $1.50 for *the whole thing* gave them a superiority over those who came in at the front gate and had to stop and pay.

Every session of Chautauqua had its quota of special days, and this year the big day was Bryan Day. The Gloriosa *Silver Bugle* prophesied that even Assembly Hall's capacity would be strained to take care of those who came to hear William Jennings Bryan. His third defeat last year as Democratic candidate for president had made no difference to his audiences. Some prominent family in Gloriosa would entertain him for dinner and bask in glory for a year. On Lou Emma's season ticket Bryan Day was marked in red.

Maddy, Eppie, and Vinnie came back with a

bucket of water. "There's a new sign at the front. 'Autos Go Slow.' " "That stuck-up Adelaide Moss's here. Ha!"

They climbed to the front seat, shoving Lou Emma over. Vinnie carried Joy, a wide-eyed red-haired doll.

"Twenty-eight people got off the last street-car."

"The Christian Endeavor's got a soda pop stand."

"Did you see anybody we know?" Lou Emma asked cautiously.

"She wants to know if Tommy's here, but she won't go look," Maddy said.

"I do not. I merely wondered who . . ."

"Tommy's here," Vinnie told her. "Him and his gang. And Miz Biddle's in charge of the Temperance Society. Wouldn't that frost you?"

"Hand Joy down," Mrs. Wacker said. "My cot's ready, so she can take her nap. We're all fixed, Professor, and I don't know how to thank you."

"I think I'm the one to do the thanking." Professor Miller put his coat on over his wet shirt. "Now girls . . . Lou Emma, Maddy . . . "

"Yes, Papa," they said apprehensively. He laughed at their faces.

"Absolutely all I was going to say was, 'Have a good time.' Goodbye."

They climbed out of the auto and all of them stood waving as he drove the Great Smith slowly down the

street. Grownups, children, baby buggies, and stray
dogs scattered before him. "Oo-*oo*-gah . . . oo-*oo*-gah
. . . oo-*oo*-gah."

As the sound of the Great Smith's horn grew fainter,
Lou Emma suddenly realized she wouldn't see her
father for *two weeks*. He had never been separated
from the girls that long before.

Tramping the grounds with Maddy, Eppie, and
Vinnie, Lou Emma found plenty to see and think
about to keep her from missing her father. Farm
wagons were unloading families and provisions; a
yellow hack arrived from the Santa Fe Chautauqua
Special Excursion. There was a fountain and a lily
pond. A steady crunch, crunch of feet on gravel made
an undertone to the rumbling of wheels and the
shouts of men struggling with tents. It became a game
to find familiar Gloriosa faces in the crowds of
strangers. They stamped them, as they stamped white
horses, licking a finger, touching a palm, and smack-
ing it down with a fist.

"Stamp for Miss Mamie Tibbetts," Eppie called,
and said behind her hand, "She's got a new switch and
it don't match her old hair very good."

"Cordy Jackson with her mother trailing her,"
Maddy stamped. "I'd sure hate to be trailed after that
way."

"There's Mr. Garrett, down on Grant Street," Lou Emma pointed.

"Who's that with him?" Maddy said.

"That's Hardy Garrett, his only son," Vinnie said. "He'll get all Mr. Garrett's money when he dies, only Mama says Hardy'll likely go first the way he drives those fast horses. I think Hardy's *cute*."

Lou Emma stared at the young man in the white linen suit, and the straw boater with a striped band. "Do we stamp for Hardy?"

"Stamp twice," Vinnie giggled. "He's the biggest catch in town."

At that moment Mrs. Biddle sailed up. "Just the girls I want to see."

"Mur-der," Maddy muttered. "We're in for it now."

"The Temperance Society has been asked to present a special drill on Bryan Day. On the big platform in Assembly Hall. Isn't that wonderful?"

There was no reply, but Mrs. Biddle didn't seem to need one. "Drill costumes will be white dresses with silver sashes and silver wands. Boys to wear white shirts, blue knickers, silver belts and swords. Practice at Willard Hall, right after Morning Devotion. I'm counting on you girls."

Away Mrs. Biddle went, gravel spurting backward from her shoes.

" 'I'm counting on you girls.' " Maddy mimicked. "Mur-der."

"I think it'll be fun," Lou Emma said.

"Me, too," Vinnie said.

Surprisingly, Eppie deserted Maddy and joined them. "Me, too. I was in a drill at school one time and I was Leader."

"Three from our tent's plenty," Lou Emma said. "If Maddy don't want to come maybe we can get Adelaide Moss."

"Who said I wasn't coming?" Maddy did one of her quick about-faces. "Madelaide Mish-mash-Moss makes me siccck."

"On the big platform, with Mr. Bryan," Eppie said. "Let's tell Mama."

They ran through the crowd, dodging people, jumping tent ropes. Mrs. Wacker was getting supper. When she heard the news she almost dropped Joy into a bowl of applesauce.

"My land o'love! Think of it! Our first day at Chautauqua."

"We'd better hurry to be on time for the First Night Program," Maddy said. "We want to get on the front bench. All the Gloriosa kids sit there."

"Set the table while I fry the ham." Mrs. Wacker tossed Joy to Eppie, who handed her to Lou Emma, who put her in the lap of Vinnie, who put Joy into the high-chair.

All four girls began to put things on the table, bumping into each other, dropping silverware in the dirt. No one cared that the butter was melted to a yellow puddle or that they had only half enough glasses.

"Water-for-two—oh—water-for-two," chanted Lou Emma, filling the glasses and putting one between each two places at the table.

The smell of their frying ham mingled with the smell of summer sausage from the next tent and the smell of frying onions from the tent beyond. A walnut leaf drifted down to decorate the applesauce. The whole meal was flavored with excitement. Lou Emma, sharing a box for a chair with Vinnie, felt that the world was perfect, like a golden apple, like a pink balloon.

"Don't know where we'll put Kate when she comes," Mrs. Wacker said.

"She's decided not to come," Vinnie said dramatically. "She's run off and got married . . . to Hardy Garrett."

The water-for-two glass tipped over. A stream of water ran down the oil-cloth and filled Vinnie's lap. She jumped up and stamped her foot.

"Lou Emma, you clumsy! You've ruint my dress."

"You'll dry out," Mrs. Wacker soothed her. "But why'd you say a thing like that about Kate? Even in fun?"

"Well, I saw Hardy 'n' Miss Kate having sodas in Berkemyer's Ice Cream Parlor," Vinnie defended herself.

"That's a long ways from getting married," her mother reproved her. "Your tongue wags too loose. More ham, Lou Emma?"

Unable to answer, Lou Emma shook her head. The food in her mouth turned to sawdust. She wouldn't even apologize for getting Vinnie's dress wet.

"Oo-*oo*-gah! Oo-*oo*-gah!"

The whole table turned. Joy chuckled happily. The Great Smith was coming around the corner. At the wheel sat Professor Miller and beside him in all the glory of her newest hat . . . pheasant feathers on wheat-gold straw . . . was Miss Kate.

Miss Kate had to be shown the tent. The "Kansas dresser" contrived from two boxes, a board, and a cretonne curtain; the hooks on the center pole for hanging clothes; the wavy mirror that must not be touched

lest it fall; the six cots . . . Joy slept with her mother;
the "dining room and kitchen" under the walnut trees.

"It's splendid," Miss Kate said. "I don't see how you
did it."

Mrs. Wacker beamed. "No room for disagreements, anyway."

"I'll live out of my suitcase," Miss Kate said. "My ironing board and iron can stay in the kitchen unless it rains."

"Ironing board? Iron?" the girls whooped.

"I can have more fun if my skirt's not wrinkled," Miss Kate said.

"I can bring out anything you need," Professor Miller said.

Lou Emma plucked at his linen duster. "I thought I wouldn't even see you for two weeks, Papa. I thought you wanted peace, quiet, and order."

"It's this way, Lou Emma. Too much peace, quiet, and order at one time might unsettle me. I'm not used to them."

"Are you going to buy a season ticket and come out every night?"

"No, no, a single admission once in a while is all I'll have time for. But tonight I wanted to see that you were properly settled. And as Kate was coming, too, it seemed only logical for me to bring her with me."

A slow, tidal movement of tenters had begun, all heading for Assembly Hall. Many of them had been coming to Chautauqua for years, and greetings were called and friendships renewed. As the crowd came in sight of Assembly Hall they hurried a little faster.

"Tommy an' J.T. an' Harris are on the front bench," Vinnie grumbled. "There's no room for us. We'll have to sit on the second."

By doing a little swapping with other girls, they managed to get on the second bench, right behind Tommy's gang. Not a boy turned around or spoke, but after the girls were seated activity on the front bench picked up.

"Pass it on," J.T. started an elbow-nudge. "You guys, pass it on."

The nudge went down and back. Tommy started an Indian pinch.

"Boys are terrible," Vinnie said, "the way they act."

" 'Boys are terrible,' " Harris trilled. "Pass it on, guys, 'Boys are terrible, the way they act.' "

"I could die," Vinnie said, her face crimson.

Now the electric lights on the grounds and in Assembly Hall were turned on. In moments clouds of insects gathered. Palm leaf fans whacked at the buzzing creatures. Harris knocked down a June-bug and tossed it into Maddy's lap. She handed it to Eppie. "Pass it on." Up and down the second bench went the unfortunate June-bug creating squeals, giggles, and shrieks. An old lady with white china teeth rapped Maddy's back with her fan.

"Put that thing down. This instant."

"Yes, ma'am." Maddy was startled into obeying.

"Yah, yah, yah," Tommy jeered, not looking back.

"Thomas." Without warning Mrs. Biddle descended on the front bench. Tommy shrank three sizes. Lou Emma watched red creep up the back of his neck. "Remind all the boys to be at drill practice tomorrow morning, sure."

"Yessum," Tommy said glumly.

Mrs. Biddle walked back up the aisle, the dark green elegance of the Gainsborough hat from Miss Kate's Chapeaux marked by every female eye.

"Oh, Thomas. Oh you kid, Thomas," J.T. dared.

"Cut that out," Tommy snarled, "or I'll pull off your arm and beatcha to death with it."

Now came the First Night Program. Clingenfelter's Brass Band, wearing gorgeous uniforms of red and gold, paraded down the center aisle and onto the platform. Their music filled Assembly Hall and reached the rafters. Oh, how they played!

Palm leaf fans waved in time to the tunes, feet tapped. The Bandmaster seemed to direct the audience as he did his musicians. When he asked the audience to join in the old Civil War song, "Wait for the Wagon," thousands of voices nearly lifted the roof of Assembly Hall.

Wait for the wagon, wait for the wagon,
Wait for the wagon and we'll all take a ride.

The concert ended, and Clingenfelter's Brass Band marched away into the night whence they had come. For a few moments the audience sat under the spell of the music. Then parents tried to locate children and children tried to avoid parents. Young couples strolled into the shadows of the tall trees. Single admissions hurried toward the front gates; tenters walked proudly to their tents. It was nine-thirty now, quiet was expected by ten, absolute silence by eleven.

"I'm going to sleep next cot to Miss Kate," Maddy announced.

"No, I am."

"I am."

"I am."

Mrs. Wacker held up her plump hand. "We'll draw straws. Bring me the broom." She broke off straws and shuffled them. "Short straw gets the cot next to Kate."

Lou Emma drew first, her fingers trembling a little. It was the short straw.

Grumbling began at once, but Mrs. Wacker cut it off. "It's only fair. Coming to Chautauqua was Lou Emma's plan in the first place. Shuck your duds and get to sleep. Mornin' will be here before you know it."

At first Lou Emma could not sleep. Too much was going on inside of her head. Flickering pictures, like the ones at the nickelodeon, kept her awake.

Chautauqua, Chautauqua, she whispered the old Indian name over and over. *I love you, Chautauqua.*

Chapter 12

The Chautauqua ran on bells. They rang first for Morning Devotion, then for classes, for afternoon and evening programs, for vespers, and for all-quiet at night.

" 'To the tin-tin-ab-u-la-tion of the bells, bells, bells.' Edgar Allan Poe," Mrs. Wacker quoted. She was taking a morning class in American Poets. "Those bells gave me fits when we first came. Now, when I hear a bell I think about American Poets."

"I think about the Temperance Society drill," Lou Emma said.

"And I think about holding in my stomach." Miss Kate's morning class was Physical Culture. "Our teacher says ab-domen, not stomach. Our motto is,

'Hold in, hold in, your ab-do-min.' She wants us to give up corsets."

"Give up corsets?" Mrs. Wacker was horrified.

"Use our muscles instead." Miss Kate finished her ironing.

"There's a toad under Eppie's cot," Maddy reported.

"Seventh," Lou Emma marked it on the Toad List.

"He's kind of cute," Maddy held up the blinking toad. "Let's name him Plutarch, after that picture in H-O-G. He'll be our tent mascot. Hi, Plutarch."

Miss Kate produced a box and Maddy punched holes in the top so Plutarch could breathe and urged all of them to collect bugs for him. "I'll bet nobody on old stuck-up Grant Street has as good a tent mascot as ours."

"Whoops! We'll be late to class." Miss Kate brushed her hair quickly and coiled it into a Figure Eight.

"How do you do it, Kate?" Mrs. Wacker asked admiringly. "Step out of this tent looking like you'd stepped out of a bandbox every mornin'."

"Nothing but good business," Miss Kate said. "I've had three orders for hats from the Physical Culture class. The teacher wants a Gainsborough."

It was more than good business, Lou Emma knew. It was soap, water, starch, sachet, hair-brushing, and everlasting ironing.

Mrs. Wacker hoisted Joy onto her arm. "I'm off to class. Joy took a real fancy to Edgar Allan Poe, poor man. Hope she likes James Russell Lowell. Don't give up corsets, Kate."

"I won't. Not as long as coatsuits are in style. Lou Emma, please bring my notebook and we'll walk over together."

It was heavenly to walk to class with Miss Kate. To carry her notebook and feel that nothing in the world could come between them. Lou Emma caught the scent of roses. She knew, now, that it came from the satin sachets Miss Kate pinned to her corset-cover, and knowing such a thing made it seem even nicer.

Mrs. Biddle was waiting to start drill practice. She had already explained that the drill was not only to show off for William Jennings Bryan, but to illustrate the differences in the good life and the other kind. Turns to the *left* in the drill meant failure to keep the pledge that every member of the Temperance Society had signed. A Pledge not to use alcohol or tobacco. Turns to the *right* were victories over temptation. The drill ended with a Grande Finale in which each member turned *right,* and stood with upraised wand or sword.

"Whoever wrote that drill must have been crazy," Maddy said this morning. "Everybody's got to turn left once in a while. If we turned right from our tent we'd end up in the river."

Mrs. Biddle smiled patiently. "Things that stand for other things are called symbols. In our drill left is wrong, and right is . . . uh . . . right."

"Well, whoever wrote the drill . . . "

"I wrote the drill," Mrs. Biddle said.

Lou Emma's skin crawled with embarrassment. Luckily, J.T. tripped one of the Thomson twins and Mrs. Biddle had to by-pass Maddy's remark.

The first practice ended in a mess. The second was worse.

"How'd you remember this stuff?" Tommy complained to Lou Emma. "I get mixed up and Ma gets mad . . . humpin'-jumpin'-jackrabbits."

"I'll tell you if you won't tell her," Lou Emma said, and explained. "In the Bible it says that goats go to the left and sheep to the right. Remember?" He nodded. "Well, when we're s'posed to turn left I think 'Swish.' Only I try not to think too hard or your mother might catch on and find him."

"For the right turns do you think 'Sheep?' "

"No, just 'Swish' and 'Not Swish.' "

Mrs. Biddle rapped for attention, "Boys and girls, places. Once more."

"It is easier," Tommy reported. "Hep, hep, hep-hep-hep, shoot that Swish if he don't keep step."

"Shhh. Your mother might hear you and ask where Swish is."

The system of "Swish" and "Not Swish" worked so well that Lou Emma was able to learn the drill quickly while the others were lost in the maze. On the first day Adelaide had been appointed Leader and her general bossiness didn't help. Mrs. Biddle made frantic changes that only confused things more.

"I don't know what Mr. Bryan is going to think," she said wearily as the Temperance Society drooped before her. "You're in the wrong place at the right time, or the right place at the wrong time."

"That Miller girl gets the hang of it better'n the rest," the pianist said. "Why don't you try her for Leader?"

Mrs. Biddle looked doubtful. "I suppose we could try."

Adelaide swelled up like a poisoned pup. "It won't do any good. The rest of 'em are all out of step."

Maddy said, "Adelaide's left-handed, maybe she's left-footed, too."

"We need a left-handed girl to present Mr. Bryan a bouquet," Mrs. Biddle said thoughtfully. "Step over here, Adelaide. We'll see how Lou Emma gets along as Leader."

Clammy sweat broke out on Lou Emma's palms. She turned to Maddy.

"Tell Mrs. Biddle I can't. Tell her I'm scared."

"Go on. You can do better'n Adelaide." Maddy shoved her forward.

Mrs. Biddle nodded to the pianist. "And-one, and-two, and-three . . ."

The music took charge of Lou Emma's feet. *Swish. Not Swish. Swish.* Behind her the rest of the Temperance Society fell into line.

"Thank heaven!" Mrs. Biddle mopped her face with her handkerchief.

"Thank Lou Emma," Maddy muttered. "That'd be more like it."

"I don't think my mother wants me handing a bouquet to William Jennings Bryan," Adelaide said. "My father's a Republican Committeeman."

"*I* will speak to your mother," Mrs. Biddle said. "Tomorrow Lou Emma Miller starts as Leader. Drill practice dismissed."

With the other girls Lou Emma hurried to Nature Study class. The lesson was on Kansas birds, but not one word penetrated the rosy haze around her. She couldn't have told a Tufted Titmouse from a Great Blue Heron.

She was *Leader*.

The night program was the Chalk Talk Man. He stood laughing and making jokes and talking to the

audience while his hands moved over sheets of paper
on an easel and, lo . . . there was a picture. George
Washington, or a Kansas wheatfield, a church at sun-
set, or the Battle of Manila Bay. Lou Emma liked best
the picture of an apple orchard in full bloom. It made
her remember Ohio, and she told Vinnie she wished
she had it to keep.

At the end the Chalk Talk Man took all his pictures
and sailed them out into the crowd. The boys on the
front bench got more than anyone.

"Boys get everything," Eppie complained.

"Wait'll us Suffragettes get Votes for Women,"
Maddy said. "Then see."

They collected bugs for Plutarch and fed him until
he would eat no more. Miss Kate was brushing her
hair its nightly one hundred strokes. Mrs. Wacker
voted the Chalk Talk Man the best yet. It didn't seem
possible, but the Chautauqua programs got better
every day.

"Tomorrow night don't sound like much," Eppie
grumbled. "A man with colored slides is going to lecture on Ancient Greece and Rome."

"Ninety-six, ninety-seven, ninety-eight, ninety-nine,
one hundred." Miss Kate flung her head upward and
the soft brown hair settled around her shoulders.
"Maybe we should tell Professor Miller about this
program."

Lou Emma consulted the list of events. "He's a professor from Yale. Papa went to Yale."

"Don't tell Papa. He'd start talking about history textbooks and talk till the cows come home," Maddy said. "Let me braid your hair, Miss Kate."

They gathered around, giggling, as Maddy tried a four-strand braid. The bell rang and Mrs. Wacker blew out the lamp. Last night the cross-patch in the next tent had rapped on the canvas wall for quiet. Warning each other, between gales of giggles, they found their cots in the dark.

"You'll laugh out of the other side of your mouth when those folks next tent call the Marshal," Mrs. Wacker warned them. "Already one young sport's been put off the grounds for smoking cigarettes."

Even this seemed funny and they kept on laughing. Sure enough, from the next tent came a sharp rap and a loud, "Quiet!"

"All right," Mrs. Wacker said. "I warned you. Don't come running to me when the Marshal takes you in."

Gradually the tent became quiet. Mrs. Wacker's breathing burbled into a snore. Plutarch thumped against the top of his box. Lou Emma turned her head on the pillow and heard a strange crackling under it. A sheet of folded paper? Stepping softly from her cot, through the crowded tent, she went to the outdoor kitchen. In the tin matchbox by the stove she

found a match and scratched it. The tiny bright flame
showed up the pink and white beauty of an apple orchard in full bloom.

Tommy had heard her tell Vinnie she wanted it,
and in some way, known only to boys, he had "traded
up" and got it. He must have raced ahead and put
it under her pillow, knowing it was hers by the L.E.M.
Miss Kate had stencilled there.

The match burned down and scorched Lou Emma's
fingers. She dropped it to the ground, but even in the
dark the pink and white apple trees still bloomed.

The afternoon was so hot that after the program
Mrs. Wacker decreed a nap. The girls grumbled a
little, but dropped down on their cots. Miss Kate
was not there.

"Bet she's over to Lovers' Lane with Hardy,"
Vinnie said.

"Lavinia Ramona Wacker, the idea!"

"Aw, Mama, I was only . . . "

"Do your only-ing on some other subject."

A lot Vinnie knew, Lou Emma told herself. Or
. . . did she?

"I don't care what Mama says," Vinnie whispered.
"Miss Kate's got a bee in her bonnet about you-know-
who."

Lou Emma turned her head away. The crackling of

the folded picture she had replaced under her pillow gave her some small comfort.

Miss Kate arrived with her arms full of ears of corn. A farmer who had come in with a load of produce had sold her all she could carry for a quarter. Lou Emma gave Vinnie a superior smile.

They sat in a circle outside the tent to husk the corn. Mrs. Wacker gave her book of American Poets to Miss Kate. "You read tomorrow's lesson on Henry Wadsworth Longfellow out loud and I'll do your share of corn huskin'. I'm slower'n a frozen tick at reading, but I'm a real fast listener."

> *By the shores of Gitchee Gumee,*
> *By the shining Big Sea Water,*
> *Stood the wigwam of Nokomis,*
> *Daughter of the Moon, Nokomis . . .*

The music of the poem fitted Miss Kate's voice and she read on and on while the corn was husked, silked, and put to cook in boiling water. The heat slacked off a little and a wandering breeze carried the spicy aroma of peach pies Mrs. Wacker had baked earlier. Leaning against the box where Miss Kate sat reading Lou Emma dreamed over the story, imagined her father as Hiawatha, and Miss Kate, a feather in her brown braids, as Minnehaha.

For supper they ate corn on the cob until they groaned, and went on eating. Their plates were stacked with the "bones of the corn" as Maddy called the cobs. Every chin was shining with butter. Mrs. Wacker brought out the pie.

"I'm too full even for peach pie," Miss Kate began scraping up plates. "After the dishes I'm going for a walk or I'll go to sleep on Ancient Greece and Rome. Save my piece of pie and I'll eat it before bed time."

"Go for your walk now, Kate," Mrs. Wacker said. "Let the girls do dishes."

Doing dishes at home was tiresome, but at Chautauqua it was fun. Maddy washed, sure that she could keep ahead of three driers. Soapy water flew, dish towels snapped. Lou Emma put Miss Kate's peach pie in a box to keep it safe.

"Finished." Maddy flung the dishcloth onto a tree branch. "Let's feed Plutarch the corn worm we saved for him."

But the corn worm was too big for the toad, who only blinked at it.

"We'd better dress. It's close to program time," Vinnie said.

"My bunion hurts." Mrs. Wacker rubbed her foot. "A sign of rain, sure."

"Where's Miss Kate?" Lou Emma asked. "We can't go without her."

"Now girls," Mrs. Wacker said, "stop pestering Kate. She puts up with it awful nice but nobody wants kids breathin' down their necks all the time."

"You always want to know where we are and what we're doin'," Eppie said.

"That's different. Kate's grown, over twenty-one."

"Over twenty-six," Maddy said. "She told us so herself."

"Then keep it to yourself," Mrs. Wacker said tartly. "And remember, Kate's free to come 'n' go with who she wants to."

Soberly, Lou Emma looked into the mirror as she smoothed her hair. *But, s'pose Miss Kate started coming and going with . . .*

"Give me a chance," Maddy shoved her away from the mirror.

"Watch out for Pluto's box," Mrs. Wacker warned.

"Oh Mama, you won't ever call him by his right name." Eppie rescued the toad and removed him to the kitchen. "Don't forget. Plutarch's outside."

"Oo-*oo*-gah!"

"It's the Great Smith." The girls trampled each other to be first to greet Professor Miller.

Chug-chug-chug-chug. The four-cylinder gasoline engine came closer, its steady, regular stroke like the beat of a faithful heart. Chug-chug-chug-chug.

Chuff-chuff-chuff-chuff. It was another sound, like

nothing Lou Emma had heard so she wasn't prepared
for what she saw when Vinnie whirled her around
to face a second auto, approaching from the other
direction. A white Stanley Steamer, the model called
the Gentleman's Speedy Roadster. In the driver's seat
with an air of happy confidence sat Hardy Garrett.
Beside him was Miss Kate.

It's not fair, Lou Emma screamed inside herself.
It's not fair.

"Told you so," Vinnie chortled. "Told you so."

"Of all the gold-plated nerve," Maddy said. "Who does he think he is?"

Eppie said, "He's Hardy Garrett, and his father owns . . . "

"Oh, shut up!" Maddy snapped.

The two autos came nearer. They were like two gladiators in the arena, maneuvering for the best place. The Stanley Steamer swerved to the right, a small jet

of steam coming from its exhaust. The Great Smith coughed, slewed to the left, and roared a challenge. Inches separated the noses of the two machines. Both drivers jerked hard on their hand brakes. Under the bright metal hoods the engines snarled. There was no chance to pass in the narrow street.

"What'll they do?" Lou Emma asked nervously.

Maddy clenched her fists. "The Great Smith'll *ram* that dude."

"Told you so," Vinnie said again.

Scarcely knowing what she did, Lou Emma slapped Vinnie's face.

With blazing eyes, Vinnie came at her and slapped Lou Emma's face so hard her back teeth jarred. With all her strength, Lou Emma returned the blow but to her horror she hit Miss Kate, who had jumped from the Gentleman's Speedy Roadster and rushed between the two girls.

Mrs. Wacker handed Joy to Eppie. "Go on, Kate. I'll handle this."

Vinnie said, "She hit me first. You saw her, Mama."

"I saw her and I heard you," Mrs. Wacker said. "Howdy, Professor."

Lou Emma could not look at her father. She stared at the ground that wavered uncertainly. His shoes needed polishing; somehow that made her want to cry.

"Lou Emma? Vinnie?" he asked in a worried voice. "What happened?"

"She hit me first," Vinnie said doggedly.

"But you were best friends. I don't understand it."

"Don't try," Mrs. Wacker advised him. "Just leave it be."

"But Lou Emma . . . she's such a good, gentle child."

Up came Lou Emma's head. "I am *not* a child."

Hardy Garrett sauntered to them, smiling. His white linen suit was spotless, his straw boater jaunty. His shoes polished. "Good evening, all."

After a slight hesitation Mrs. Wacker said, "Howdy, Hardy. Make you acquainted with Professor Cyrus Miller from up to the college."

It shocked Lou Emma to see the two shake hands. Maddy sniffed.

"Glad to meet you, Professor. I'm indebted to you, you might say."

"Oh? In what way?" Professor Miller inquired politely.

"The day you chased our cows over half the county, Dad got so mad trying to round 'em up that he said no plague-taken college professor . . . no offense meant . . . was going to get ahead of the Garretts. Next day he ordered the Stanley. I'd been after him to do it for months."

"Well, well," Professor Miller said. "If I'd known I'd have advised you to get a Great Smith. Any time you'd like to check your engine's capacity the Great Smith and I will be happy to accommodate you."

Hardy laughed good naturedly. "That wouldn't be fair. The Gentleman's Speedy Roadster is a special job. Dad always gets the best."

"I'll get my hat," Miss Kate said hurriedly.

"You don't need a hat, Kate," Hardy said.

"I wouldn't think of going out with a well-dressed man like you without a hat," Miss Kate said, and turned to the others. "Hardy's taking me for a little spin in his new auto."

"You'll miss the program," Maddy said, aghast.

But Miss Kate went into the tent without answering. Hardy called after her. "Don't forget that piece of peach pie you promised me."

"We'll take it with us." Miss Kate's voice was muffled.

She's getting dressed up. It's not fair.

Lou Emma was seething. Hardy was going to get the peach pie she had saved in a box for Miss Kate. Something clicked in her mind. *Not if I can help it.*

"I got the Stanley up to thirty-two at the Fair Grounds," Hardy said.

"Good try," Professor Miller nodded. "But a gasoline engine . . ."

"Stands to reason steam's better," Hardy said. "Look at the railroads."

"The Great Smith was the first auto to climb Pike's Peak," Vinnie said, her face as red as her hair. Lou Emma knew this was Vinnie's way of making up. She put her arm around Vinnie and looked at Hardy.

"And Pike's Peak's a lot taller than Kansas," she said.

"I can't argue with that," Hardy said. "But aren't you the two that were fighting, tooth and toenail, when we drove up?"

"Lou Emma is my best friend," Vinnie said with dignity.

" 'A friend loveth at all times,' Psalms 17:17," Lou Emma said.

"Well I'll be doggoned." Hardy fanned himself with his straw boater.

Miss Kate came out of the tent. She had changed to her best white shirtwaist and her pink linen skirt, but it was her hat that hardened Lou Emma's heart and made her determined to carry out her idea. Miss Kate was wearing the white hat with three pink roses that the Miller girls had first seen from the cottonwood tree. *The very hat.*

"I'll get your piece of peach pie; I put it in a box to keep it safe," Lou Emma said. She put the box carefully on the floor of the Stanley Steamer.

It was a subdued group of tenters that made their way to Assembly Hall. Only Joy was happy as she bounced on her mother's arm.

"That dude!" Maddy burst out. "And Lou Emma, you ought to be ashamed serving him peach pie. And Miss Kate ought to be ashamed, too."

"No more of that," Professor Miller said sternly. "Kate has a right to do as she pleases."

"I told 'em that," Mrs. Wacker said, "but they think they own her. If only you'd said you were coming tonight. If you'd sent word, Professor."

"I didn't plan to come until I read in the *Silver Bugle* that Dr. Robert Barnes of Yale is the speaker. I knew Bob Barnes in college."

Mrs. Wacker stopped, blocking the aisle. "Girls! Girls! Girls! Professor Miller's personally acquainted with the speaker. Wait till I tell 'em that in American Poets."

Dr. Robert Barnes of Yale was a short, chunky man who looked more like a clerk in a dry-goods store than a famous author, traveler, and professor. But when he began to speak, even the front bench was pin-drop quiet. In spite of her troubles Lou Emma found she was listening. Rome, Athens, Sparta, Carthage became as real as Cleveland, Ohio; as Topeka, Kansas.

The lights were turned out and colored slides

trembled onto the screen. Tag-ends of lines her father
had quoted came to her.

*The glory that was Greece, the grandeur that was
Rome . . .*

There it was. The wine-dark sea of Homer, the
Forum, the Colosseum. It was real. No wonder her
father loved history and loved to talk to them about
it. H-O-G was more than a big fat green book; it was
a part of the world. Gibbon's *Decline and Fall of the
Roman Empire* was about actual people. She would
never complain about Gibbon again. The Plain of
Marathon was the next slide. With a thrill, Lou Emma
recognized it for what it must be before Dr. Barnes
told them.

*The Mountains look on Marathon, and Marathon
looks on the sea . . .*

The lights came on. The audience blinked, sighed,
took up its palm leaf fans and returned to Gloriosa,
Kansas.

They drove Dr. Barnes to the depot so that he could
catch the night Santa Fe for Denver. He was, Mrs.
Wacker whispered, as comfortable as an old shoe. He
beamed at all of them, admired the Great Smith,
called Professor Miller "Skinny," and reminded him
of the time they got arrested on a Glee Club trip.

"Stop it," Professor Miller grinned. "I have to uphold discipline with the girls after you've gone. But that lecture was a credit to Old Eli, Bob. I wish my Greek and Roman History Classes at EKCC could hear it."

"Later," Dr. Barnes promised. "Now I'm finishing a textbook. Get your classes to use it, Skinny. Much better than my lectures."

"Same old Bob. Always an eye to the main chance," Professor Miller said. "But I'll look it over. I have some ideas of my own about textbooks."

Lou Emma and Maddy moaned as the talk started, but the whistle of the Santa Fe cut it short. Dr. Barnes climbed aboard and they waved him out of sight.

The night watchman at the gate grumbled as he let them in.

"Dare you to ask if a Stanley Steamer's come in," Vinnie said.

"Papa'd eat me alive," Lou Emma refused the dare. It's bound to've. Miss Kate knows the rules. We had special permission because of Dr. Barnes' train time."

But when they reached the tent the cot next to Lou Emma's was empty.

Mrs. Wacker's bunion had been right. By morning rain was streaming onto a drowned Chautauqua grounds. A drip-drip-drip hit Lou Emma's nose and she waked to find the tent leaking in three spots. A

stream of water flowed under their cots and on out
the back. The dresser was piled with food as Mrs.
Wacker and Miss Kate tried to salvage their supplies.

Breakfast was bread and milk eaten hunched up on
the cots. The milk was blinky. Vinnie poured hers
into the stream running through the tent.

No one mentioned Miss Kate's absence of last
night.

Maddy peered out at the rain. "What are we going to do?"

"You're not sugar nor salt. You won't melt," Miss Kate said.

"Rain before seven, shine before eleven," Eppie said wisely.

"That's right," Mrs. Wacker agreed. "I vote we go ahead as usual."

"I always feed Plutarch after I eat," Maddy said. "I'll do it now."

Lou Emma's heart stepped up its beating.

"Where's Plutarch's box?" Maddy rummaged through the things on the dresser. "I hope the poor thing wasn't left out in the rain."

"I wisht all I had to worry about was leavin' a toad out in the rain," Mrs. Wacker said. "Remember? Eppie set him out last night."

Maddy darted into the downpour. She gave a wild scream that left them open-mouthed, then she came dashing back with the box. Inside it was a soggy, rain-soaked piece of peach pie.

"Jerusalem my happy home!" Maddy gasped. "Lou Emma . . . you . . . you . . . "

"Lou Emma gave Hardy the wrong box, *by mistake*," Miss Kate said.

There was an instant of stunned silence, broken only by the drumming of the rain on the tent. Then they laughed and laughed and laughed until tears came and they were breathless. Even Miss Kate laughed, Lou Emma noticed uneasily.

"I oughtn't to laugh thisaway," Mrs. Wacker wiped her eyes on the hem of her skirt. "But I'd give a pretty to've seen Hardy when he opened up that box and saw old Pluto."

"Plutarch, Mama."

"All right, Plutarch. What'd he do, Kate?"

"He laughed, the same way you did. Then he turned Plutarch loose," Miss Kate said. "I'm afraid we've lost our mascot, girls."

"But wasn't Hardy mad?" Vinnie asked, big-eyed.

"Oh no, he thought it was funny. But neither of us had had dessert so . . . " she paused and Lou Emma felt Miss Kate's eyes on her. "So he took me to Berkemyers and we had Double Chocolate Fluffs."

"Double?" Eppie's tongue circled her lips.

"Double," Miss Kate said firmly. "Then we decided to drive to Waycross."

Waycross? Waycross is nine miles from Gloriosa.

Once, back in Auden, Lou Emma received a boomerang for her birthday. It took a week to learn to throw it, and when she did the hateful thing sailed back and hit her in the stomach. She remembered how it felt, and she knew, now, that her idea was the same thing. A boomerang.

Chapter 13

The hurt from the boomerang Lou Emma got for her birthday had been gone in five minutes. The hurt from the boomerang of her plan to embarrass Hardy and show Miss Kate she shouldn't go out with him, went on and on. It wasn't as if Miss Kate acted mad at Lou Emma. It was more as if Lou Emma was mad at herself.

She saw, now, what a bone-headed thing it had been to do. It was almost as if she had suggested that they take a spin to Waycross, or go to Berkemyers for Double Chocolate Fluffs. And never one word had Miss Kate volunteered about how she got back to the tent after the gate was closed.

As the days went by Lou Emma became more and more unhappy. She got her feelings hurt over nothing. The Chautauqua programs no longer seemed wonderful. She went to sleep on the lecture, *Woman: Her Place in State, Church, and Home* that Maddy thought was best of all. She didn't like the English Opera Singers, or the elocutionist who recited James Whitcomb Riley's poems. Vinnie began going around with Maddy and Eppie and at last asked back the buttons she had given Lou Emma for her charm string.

Her contrariness even drove her to cheer for the Holton team in the baseball game. And Tommy was playing First Base for Gloriosa.

Only the drill still held its charms. By using the Swish, Not Swish, system the Temperance Society was nearly perfect. At the Grand Finale Lou Emma felt her heart uplifted, along with her silver wand, and she knew she would keep her signed Pledge all her life long.

On Bryan Day the girls were to wear white organdy, dimity, or cross-barred muslin. Only Adelaide was allowed to be different. She was going to wear white satin.

"The poor girl will swelter," Miss Kate said.

Lou Emma took immediate offense. "Brides wear white satin in hot weather. They don't care, do they?"

Miss Kate gave her a level look. "I've never been a bride."

Maddy took her to task later. "Why'd you act so hateful to Miss Kate about brides? Aunt Jesse said unmarried females didn't like such questions."

"Aunt Jesse Miller is a mean old pill-er," Lou Emma chanted and made a face when Maddy looked shocked. "You made it up yourself."

"But I never meant for you to act so hateful saying it."

Lou Emma walked away.

"The nice one." "The good one." I'm sick of it. S-I-C-K.

Bryan Day was two days off. After the rain the heat had returned. The river had gone down and left wide mud flats. The sun drew the moisture and seemed to dump it right back on the people as perspiration.

Mrs. Biddle did not relax practice of the drill for one moment. "I expect the best of you, boys and girls. You represent Kansas. Never forget."

"Ad astra per aspera," Lou Emma muttered and marshaled them through the complex maze once again.

The morning of Bryan Day the heat was so great it was hard to breathe.

"Land o' love," Mrs. Wacker puffed. "If it's this way before nine, what'll it be by three o'clock?"

"The ice man told Tommy William Jennings Bryan had ordered a hundred-pound cake of ice to be on the platform," Maddy said.

" 'The Passing of Plutocracy,' " Vinnie read from the handbill, advertising the lecture. "I hope it don't take long to pass, whatever it is."

"It won't seem long," Miss Kate said. "Lou Emma, I'll iron your dress."

She wanted to say "Thank you, ma'am!" Instead she said, "I do my own ironing at home, so I'll do it here."

The others stared but she refused to look at them. As she slid her white dress over the ironing board she caught a glimpse of Mrs. Wacker shaking her head and Miss Kate shrugging her shoulders.

When she had finished the dress she laid it carefully on her cot and walked away from the tent.

"Practice is at ten, sharp," Maddy called after her. "Girls only. Biddles are having Mr. Bryan to supper at their house and she's gone home to see about things. She said not to come any earlier than ten."

"I'm not going to practice," Lou Emma flung back. "I'm only going to get away from this silly tent."

"Well, good riddance to bad rubbish!" Maddy flared.

Lou Emma neither looked back nor answered. She began to run, aimlessly, as if she might outrun her unhappy thoughts. She found herself at Lovers

Lane and walked slowly down the little path that led to the river's edge. She sat down on the bench where it was said that couples sat to spoon.

Why did I say that to Miss Kate about brides and white satin?

Her head ached and the glare from the river hurt her eyes. She leaned forward, elbows on her knees, head in her hands. Something was under the bench. Automatically she pulled it out. A package of cigarettes, opened.

"Already some young sport's been put off the grounds for smoking cigarettes," Mrs. Wacker had said. Perhaps this was the very spot the Marshal had caught him. She felt sorry for the unknown young man; he must be as miserable as she was. Should she throw the cigarettes into the river?

No. She would save them for Swish. Swish deserved something extra for without him she would never have become Leader. She dropped the package into her pocket and sat swinging her feet, thinking about Swish.

The last drill practice was over. Next would be the performance itself . . . on the big platform. The time that had once been dim and distant now was rushing on them. It was ten-thirty A.M.; two thirty P.M. was the hour.

Mrs. Biddle spoke impressively. "Girls, this is a

day you will never forget. You will share the platform with the Great Commoner, himself."

"My Aunt Jesse says it isn't nice to be common," Maddy said.

"As I have told you, Maddy, Commoner is only a *symbol*. The turns in our drills are *symbols* of the way we intend to keep our Pledge."

Adelaide Moss's hand shot up. "S'pose a girl pretends to keep the Pledge but she don't. Really."

"I am sure that none of *our* girls . . ."

"Yes ma'am. One of our girls."

Mrs. Biddle frowned. "No girl who breaks our Pledge not to use alcohol or tobacco in any form can continue in our Temperance Society. But you must be mistaken and you really should not say such things."

"S'pose she had cigarettes in her pocket this very minute?" Adelaide said, eyes bright with malice. "S'pose she was the Leader of the drill."

A gasp, then a terrible silence. In the suffocating heat it was as if all of them had been frozen.

It can't be happening. It can't.

"Don't you dare talk about my sister that way!" Maddy started for Adelaide but Mrs. Biddle's arm held her back.

"This is a serious matter Adelaide. Do you have proof?"

Without a word Adelaide reached over and jerked the opened package of cigarettes from Lou Emma's pocket. "What do you call that?"

"Lou Emma?" Mrs. Biddle whispered. Her arm dropped as if she no longer had the strength to hold it up. "Lou Emma Miller?"

If Mrs. Biddle had screamed at her, or even grabbed her and shaken her, Lou Emma could have stood it better. Her shocked whisper and the look of absolute unbelief on Maddy's face was too heavy to bear. She gulped, hard.

"They're not mine. Not really. They're for . . ." Lou Emma stopped, realizing that if she said the cigarettes were for Swish Mrs. Biddle would know where he was hidden and come and take him to the slaughterhouse.

"If they are not yours, why are they in your pocket? Remember your Pledge, Lou Emma. Speak the truth."

"But it is the truth. And I didn't break the Pledge. I wouldn't for anything in the world. They're not mine. They're for . . ." Again she stopped.

"We are waiting," Mrs. Biddle said solemnly.

Lou Emma ran. Ran faster than she ever had in her life.

Blindly, she ran toward the river. Feet pounded behind her for a while, and voices called her name, but all of that was gone now. The bell rang for classes. People would be hurrying to Nature Study, American Poets, Physical Culture. They would be talking about her. It seemed to her she could hear one enormous voice saying, "Lou Emma Miller, Professor Miller's daughter, the good one, Leader of the drill, broke her pledge. Cigarettes in her pocket. She said they weren't hers but you know . . . you know . . ."

Face down on the grass she sobbed without tears.

At last she walked down to the riverbank, her feet sliding in the mud. Once she very nearly slipped into the water but a wild grape vine was dangling overhead and she pulled up on it and swung over to the grass and walked on. A fence enclosed the Chautauqua Grounds but it was a fairly easy matter for Lou Emma to find a low spot and scootch under. She was outside now.

What am I going to do?

There was no going back to the tent. She had disgraced them all. "Good riddance to bad rubbish," Maddy had called. She was bad rubbish, all right. Miss Kate? Mrs. Wacker? No. She couldn't go back. Adelaide in her white satin would be Leader of the drill. Strangely, she didn't hate Adelaide. She walked on.

The street that led from Gloriosa to the Chautauqua was very busy. A banner crowd was coming out for Bryan Day. A farm wagon crawled to a stop beside her. It was the only thing on wheels going toward town. The driver called: "Want a ride to town, Sis?"

She nodded wordlessly and he pointed to the back of his wagon that was filled with straw. "Hop in. I took a load of watermelons in early and sold every one of 'em on the grounds. Bet there's ten thousand folks there."

Ten thousand. Lou Emma settled herself in the straw. At two-thirty P.M. ten thousand people would watch Adelaide lead the Temperance Society through the drill.

But I didn't break my Pledge. I couldn't say I did if I didn't.

The wagon jolted and rumbled in the dust. Sunk in misery, Lou Emma didn't even notice when the team stopped. "Here's where I turn off, Sis. Want me to take you home? You look a mite dauncy."

"Nossir. Thanks for the ride. It's just the heat, I guess."

"It's an all-fired hot day. You wouldn't catch me sittin' on no hard bench listenin' to Bill Bryan on a day like this. So long." He shook the reins and the wagon rumbled away.

Gloriosa was almost deserted. Everybody who could ride, walk, or crawl had gone to Bryan Day. Lou Emma plodded along the quiet street. Her feet were taking her home. What was she going to say to her father when she got there?

She went to the front window of the small brown house and looked in. Professor Miller sat in the Morris chair, intent on his study. The sight of him, plainly unaware of the disgrace she had brought on him, made everything worse. If only she could go inside and tell him.

Rule Number Two. Never Interrupt Papa When He's Studying.

Not even when Maddy jumped from the hayloft and broke Lou Emma's collar-bone had they called him from his work. She backed away from the window and walked around to the barn. Inside, in welcome shade the Great Smith stood, shining and polished, ready for Bryan Day.

"Na-a-a-a-a." Swish greeted her joyously.

"Oh Swish, darling, darling Swish." She sat on the runningboard and buried her face in the little goat's soft hide. For the first time tears slid down her cheeks. Swish licked them away. She laughed a shaky laugh.

"You silly old goat! But I'm glad I didn't tell. You're worth a million silly old drills. It's only that . . . that . . ." She didn't go on. It was enough to have Swish beside her, twitching his short, stubby tail. She was hot, tired, dirty, hungry, and in disgrace, but here was somebody who was on her side.

Time passed slowly in the barn. A kind of stoniness
settled over Lou Emma. She heard the kitchen pump
go chug-gurgle, chug-gurgle; she heard the slam of
the ice-box top. If she went in now Rule Number
Two would not be broken.

Minutes dragged on. The clock in the kitchen
struck once. Was it twelve-thirty? One? Or one-thirty?
It was hopeless to try to figure out. William Jennings
Bryan was to speak at three, the drill was at two-

thirty. Mr. Bryan's train arrived at two. Dr. and Mrs. Biddle were to meet him in their surrey. Clock faces spun in her head. What time was it now? What difference did it make?

When her father came out to get the Great Smith he would find her. He'd have to know, soon enough, but she couldn't tell him now. She looked for a place to hide; near the manger where the cow used to stay was an empty bin, once used for feed. She climbed in and squatted down. It was deathly hot. Spiders and spider nests were in the corners.

The Nature Study teacher said most spiders were harmless. She hoped these were. Arachnids, the book called spiders. Their father had told them the story of Arachne, the Greek girl so proud of her weaving that she challenged the goddess, Athene, to a contest and was changed into a spider because of her pride.

Was Lou Emma Miller punished for her pride in being Leader?

She leaned her head wearily against the dusty bin. Then she heard the rarely-used front doorbell, Whirrrr-whirrrr.

"Lou Emma?" her father's voice called. *"Lou Emma?"*

She huddled into the smallest space she could. *Not now, please.*

Voices were coming closer. They were in the barn.

"She couldn't possibly be here," Professor Miller was saying. "I've been at home all day. Why do you think she's here, Kate?"

"She's got to be," Miss Kate said. "I suppose you'd say it's logical."

"Logical? What happened? I don't understand all this."

There was a third voice. Drearily Lou Emma wondered what Mrs. Biddle could do to her now.

"I'll never forgive myself," Mrs. Biddle said. "After we found tracks leading down to the river . . . Dr. Biddle has boys diving there, right now . . . and then Kate said . . ."

"*Where is Lou Emma?*" Professor Miller shouted.

"Na-a-a-a-a," Swish bleated and rattled his chain.

"That's Thomas' goat? How did it get here? I thought . . ."

"Forget the goat," Professor Miller snapped. "Where's Lou Emma?"

"Just a minute," Miss Kate said, and Lou Emma heard the tinkle of the chain as if Swish were being let loose. "Swish, go find Lou Emma."

"That's a goat, not a bloodhound," Professor Miller stormed. "Get the sheriff, get the police, we've got to find her. Stop this goat foolishness."

Lou Emma held her breath. She heard the delicate tap of Swish's hoofs, the scrape as they rasped on the wooden bin. Turning her head up as best she could in her cramped quarters she looked into Swish's wise golden eyes.

"Na-a-a-a-a," he said, and his beard twitched. "Na-a-a-a."

She stood up, unfolding her aching legs and gave Swish a little shove. "Tattle-tale," she said.

With one swoop her father lifted her from the bin, hugging her so hard she lost her breath and choked. Miss Kate got mixed into the hug and came out with her Figure Eight hair-do looking like Zero. Professor Miller set Lou Emma down with a loving shake.

"Why didn't you tell me you'd come home?"

"Rule Number Two. Never Interrupt Papa When He's Studying."

"Heaven forgive me for being a blind, selfish, pig-headed . . ."

"Heaven forgive me," Mrs. Biddle broke in. "No, I won't put it onto heaven. Lou Emma, will you forgive me?"

Her mouth fell open and she had to swallow twice. "Yes ma'am. But I didn't break my pledge."

"I know, and I should have known it all the time. Kate Turner gave me a real talking-to. She said you'd never break a promise."

Miss Kate said that? About me?

"I think I'd better ask forgiveness of you, Mrs.

Biddle," Miss Kate said. "I wasn't very ladylike. But when Maddy called me out of Physical Culture . . . imagine doing knee-bends with the temperature 102 degrees . . . and told me about the cigarettes . . ."

"Cigarettes?" Professor Miller frowned, puzzled.

"When Maddy said Adelaide pulled a package of cigarettes out of Lou Emma's pocket, I knew they must be for Swish. But before I could locate Mrs. Biddle someone had already seen those footprints going down to the river."

"Oh . . . oh," Mrs. Biddle moaned, "I'll never forget that moment."

"But where did Lou Emma get cigarettes? I thought smoking was forbidden on the grounds."

"It is." Lou Emma thought it was her turn to talk. "Only I found a package under the bench at the end of Lovers Lane. I thought Swish ought to get'em because he showed me how to do the drill. Did you know I was Leader of the drill, Papa? I was going to surprise you, only now I guess Adelaide'll get to do it."

"You are still Leader," Mrs. Biddle said, "and when I get my hands on Adelaide Moss . . ."

"I had it coming to me," Lou Emma said. "I pushed her out first."

"You say Swish showed you how to do the drill? Do you mean he's in it?" Professor Miller asked.

Lou Emma started to explain, but Mrs. Biddle pointed an accusing finger at Swish, who had been happily chewing on Professor Miller's trouser cuffs.

"Is this where that goat's been hidden? Why didn't you tell me those cigarettes were for him?"

"I promised Tommy to keep him hid. So you wouldn't send Swish to the slaughterhouse. You won't, will you, please, Mrs. Biddle."

"I promise not to," Mrs. Biddle said, "but I promise that I am going to send Thomas Biddle to the woodshed."

Lou Emma had a feeling that this was between mother and son and she should not interfere. But after all this trouble she wanted to be sure that Swish was safe. Grownup promises have too many holes in them.

"We can keep Swish here, if you don't want him around. He can belong to Tommy but we can be his keepers. Can't we, Papa?"

"I couldn't refuse you anything today, Lou Emma. I'm lucky that all you want is to be a goat-keeper."

"And I'm sure Dr. Biddle will consider this in the service record of the History Department," Mrs. Biddle said graciously. She took the package of cigarettes from her handbag. "I do not approve of the use of tobacco, Lou Emma, but I think you have earned these for that goat."

Lou Emma took the package. "If you could call him Swish, instead of 'that goat,' and if you'd give him just one cigarette . . ."

Behind her she heard Miss Kate's muffled giggle.

"I suppose I ought to go the whole way," Mrs. Biddle said resignedly. "Here Swish, here Swish." She extended a limp, bent cigarette as if it might explode. Swish nibbled delicately at her hand. Mrs. Biddle's face was a study. From far away they heard the whistle of the Santa Fe. The remains of the cigarette dropped to the ground.

"That's William Jennings Bryan's train. I was supposed to meet it." Mrs. Biddle looked as if she might be going to cry.

"The Great Smith'll get you to the depot in time," Lou Emma said.

"Do you mean it? Really?" Mrs. Biddle stared at the big red auto.

"Certainly." Professor Miller reached for the crank. "Thirty miles an hour is only four minutes from the depot. Get in, Mrs. Biddle."

"Come on, all of you." Mrs. Biddle waved Miss Kate and Lou Emma into the back seat. She climbed in front, sitting straight as a ramrod.

Out of the barn, out of the yard, into the street they went with a clatter and a warning "Oo-*oo*-gah" to the Wacker hens. The Great Smith tore through the dust, rounding corners on two wheels—Mrs. Biddle in the front seat holding on for dear life, Lou Emma and Miss Kate in the back seat, bouncing like popcorn grains in a wire popper.

"Woo-woo-*wah-woo!*" wailed the Santa Fe, much closer now.

"Oo-*oo*-gah!" The Great Smith returned the challenge.

Professor Miller set his jaw, jerked the hand throttle to the last notch and the Great Smith lunged forward.

"Oh my soul!" Miss Kate clutched Lou Emma and they bounced together. "I'll bet Mr. Bryan . . . never had . . . a welcoming committee . . . like this one."

With brakes screaming, the Great Smith slewed to a stop as the Santa Fe steamed up to the depot. A crowd was gathered to see Mr. Bryan, but they stared instead at the throbbing red auto and the wind-whipped quartet in it. Lou Emma heard a woman say, "That *can't* be Lavinia Biddle."

Mrs. Biddle, her head held high, gave no notice to the crowd. She walked rapidly to the door of the Pullman car where Mr. Bryan had appeared. He wore the seersucker suit, Panama hat, and the black string tie that were his trademarks. He waved his hat to the crowd and smiled broadly at their cheers.

Shepherding her guest toward the Great Smith,
Mrs. Biddle informed him that the auto was made in
Topeka, Kansas. She managed to make it sound as if
it had been manufactured especially for this occasion.
Miss Kate and Professor Miller were introduced, and
then with a special flourish, "Miss Louisa Emmaline
Miller, Leader of the drill which our Temperance
Society has prepared for Bryan Day."

The introduction tied Lou Emma's tongue completely, but Mr. Bryan didn't appear to mind her
silence. He shook her hand as if he had been waiting
for years just to meet *her*. One thing she knew, now.
The Great Commoner was the symbol for something
pretty nice, and not at all what Aunt Jesse meant
when she said "common."

Ten thousand people.

They filled Assembly Hall and overflowed into the grounds. Parasols raised against the sun gave a gay, carnival look. The platform was banked with ferns from the parlors of Gloriosa. Red, white, and blue bunting draped the edge. Mr. Bryan and a half-dozen other men sat in the center of the platform, and on a table near them was the hundred-pound cake of ice Tommy had said would be there. Palm leaf fans . . . Mr. Bryan's included . . . waved so hard that the audience appeared to be in motion, like an earthquake, or a heaving ocean.

The Temperance Society waited to go on the platform. They had been washed, starched, ironed, and shoe-polished out of all recognition.

Mrs. Biddle came down the line, adjusting sashes, straightening bow ties. "Lou Emma, I am depending on you. Kansas is depending on you."

The knuckles on Mrs. Biddle's hand were white as she clutched an ivory fan. There was a trembling of the ruching on the Gainsborough hat. With a shock Lou Emma realized Mrs. Biddle was as scared as she was. "Yes ma'am," she croaked in answer.

Ad astra per aspera. Oh Swish, Swish, help me now.

Mrs. Biddle lifted her fan; the pianist's hands crashed down. Lou Emma moved forward with a jerk.

Somehow she was moving, and the rest of the Temperance Society was following. The music carried them onto the vast open space of the platform where Mr. Bryan sat at ease. She felt the little wave of coolness from the cake of ice. Mr. Bryan smiled in encouraging recognition. Lou Emma's knees stiffened. The audience was out there, like some great beast, waiting for her to make a mistake so that it could devour her. But she needn't look at the audience. She looked at Mr. Bryan. He smiled again and gave the slightest nod. Her breath came easier.

In the wings Adelaide was standing with her big bouquet of flowers and her white satin dress. The dress was sweated to her skin. Miss Kate had been right; satin was a mistake.

Miss Kate's out in the audience, watching.

Now they had reached the Wheel Within a Wheel, so the drill was half over. Lou Emma dared to steal a look at the audience. It didn't seem like a beast at all. There was the old lady with the china teeth. It became *fun* to be Leader. She began to twitch her hips on the Not Swish turns so that her blue silk sash flirted out to the best advantage.

All too quickly it was over. The Temperance Society lined up for the Grand Finale, wands and swords uplifted. They had done the drill without a mistake. Thunderous applause began to roll, reached

a mighty crescendo, and diminished. They had done
their best for Kansas!

As long as she lived Lou Emma would never forget
that she heard William Jennings Bryan. His voice
reached out over the vast audience, past the benches,
to the farthest person standing on the edge of the
crowd. It was a voice like the pipe organ at the Methodist Church. It could be high and clear, or deep and
heavy, it could make a listener laugh or cry, or stand
enthralled. As to what was the *Passing of Plutocracy*
she neither knew nor cared. It was hearing the voice
that counted.

For more than an hour the audience sat or stood in
the ghastly heat, intent on every word. At the end
they gave Mr. Bryan the famous Chautauqua Salute,
each person waving a handkerchief in the air.

It was an amazing thing to see. Ten thousand
white handkerchiefs, with here and there a red or
blue bandana. It was the greatest honor a Chautauqua speaker could receive. Health-minded people op-
posed it, saying the Salute spread germs. But Lou
Emma, waving her handkerchief high, was certain
that no germ would dare do its evil work in Mr.
Bryan's presence; it would simply wither away.

That night after the others were asleep Miss Kate

whispered to Lou Emma to come outside for a few minutes. The night was warm and above them the high walnut trees rustled in the little breeze.

"I wanted you to know that I'm proud of you, Lou Emma."

"Because of the drill? We didn't make a single mistake."

"That's only part of it. I'm proud the way you stood up for Swish, and that you didn't blame Adelaide for what she did . . . I'm sure I wouldn't have been so nice."

"Oh Miss Kate, I acted awful to you. I'm so ashamed."

"Not really awful. You got crossways with the world. That's all."

She made it simple and clear-cut. A thing that could be forgiven.

"It wasn't any fun," Lou Emma said. "I wish I hadn't of."

"It's over now." Miss Kate patted her shoulder. "Put it out of your mind. Vinnie wants you to take back the buttons for your charm string. And Maddy said she would hit anybody who called you 'bad rubbish.' "

"But she called me that herself, first off."

"I know. But Maddy loves you so much she's forgotten that." Miss Kate hesitated, then went on.

"There's one more thing. The night I went out with Hardy."

"Yes ma'am," Lou Emma said, stiffening in spite of herself.

"He had engine trouble. It was 'way after midnight when we got back. Hardy bribed the watchman to let us in. I was ashamed, terribly ashamed, for you girls to know about it."

"It wasn't your fault," Lou Emma said, suddenly light-hearted. "Everybody knows a steam engine's not as good as a gasoline engine."

"Don't tell Hardy," Miss Kate said, and laughing softly, not to wake the others, they started back into the tent. A thumping noise came from inside.

Lou Emma grabbed hold of Miss Kate. "Plutarch's ghost?"

"No, Maddy caught a new toad while we were all looking for you. She put it in a box, and named it— Lou Emma."

Chapter 14

The 1909 Chautauqua was over. The tents were stored for the next season. The gravel was raked in the streets. The lily pond was drained and the fountain tied up in an old feed sack. Gray squirrels raced across the roof of Assembly Hall. Driving past in the Great Smith, Lou Emma and Maddy looked at the ground with mournful pleasure.

"It was such fun while it was happening, I hate to think it's over," Maddy said. "What'd you like best? Very best?"

Lou Emma knew without having to search her memory. *"A Midsummer Night's Dream.* I liked Bottom with his donkey ears, and Oberon, but I liked Titania, Queen of the Fairies, best of anything at all. I wish they'd do more plays."

"Chautauqua can't put on plays," Maddy said. "The church people wouldn't like it. Chautauqua was church-started."

"How about *A Midsummer Night's Dream,* then?"

"That's Shakespeare. That's different."

"Ghost Night was fun," Lou Emma said. Ghost Night was the last night of the season when the performers were all gone and the tenters put on the program, acting as "ghosts" of the professionals.

Maddy laughed. "Remember Dr. Biddle acting like William Jennings Bryan with his palm leaf fan, and all?"

"Mrs. Biddle didn't like that," Lou Emma said, not sure that she had liked it either. "She didn't laugh once."

"Mrs. Wacker sure laughed. Eppie said she popped a corset string."

"Did you know that Miss Kate sold five hats off her head at Chautauqua and took orders for nine more?" Lou Emma gloried at the thought.

"Adelaide said her mother said it was shameful for Miss Kate to commercialize a noble institution." Maddy rolled her eyes till the whites showed.

"Mr. Moss's ice wagons sold ice on the grounds every single day," Lou Emma said hotly. "What's the difference in hats and ice?"

"Well, one melts and one doesn't," Maddy said.

"But I think Mrs. Moss was mad because Miss Kate wouldn't copy Mrs. Biddle's Gainsborough hat for her. Miss Kate said maybe in New York City, but not in Gloriosa."

"It'll be fun having Miss Kate next door," Lou Emma said.

"I've been thinking," Maddy said, slowly, "about Miss Kate . . ."

"What about her?" Lou Emma felt a quaver of excitement, the kind one of their housekeepers said came when a goose walks over your grave.

"She's twenty-six, but she doesn't really act old. Couldn't she be like our big sister?"

The excitement dried up. Lou Emma felt cheated and cross. "I've got one sister, thank you, and that's a big fat plenty."

With the beginning of the college term at hand, things at EKCC were looking much better. Cows no longer grazed on the campus. A horse-drawn mowing machine clicked along, cutting the high grass. Every window in Old Main sparkled. A new flag was on the flagpole, its forty-five stars bright in the sunlight. From Rehearsal Hall came the ping-pang-ping of the piano tuner working over the old grand piano.

"I hope Papa's classes are full up," Lou Emma said as they waited in the auto for Professor Miller.

"He sure wants a telescope for his Astronomy classes, but Dr. Biddle said 'no.' He said EKCC would have to get along on its naked eyes this year."

"Maybe he can have one next year," Lou Emma spoke hopefully.

"Next year, next year. Why does everything have to be next year? By the time next year comes it's this year and there's all that stuff waiting in line for *this* year. I like things to happen now."

"We could give the drill and charge admission and make money to buy EKCC a telescope," Lou Emma sat up straight, dazzled by her idea.

"We wouldn't make a dime," Maddy said practically. "All those people in Assembly Hall that day came to hear William Jennings Bryan, you nitwit."

The lovely idea popped in Lou Emma's face and she sat back, deflated. Her stocking was wrinkled and she took off her slipper to straighten it. There, under the lining of her slipper, was the outline of her lucky penny. The sight of it reminded her of their first day in Gloriosa, how they had gone to Miss Kate's Chapeaux, and found the hat with three pink roses.

Wish I might, wish I may, get the wish I wish today.

A great golden moon balanced on the horizon. It seemed near enough to touch. There was still daylight left in the west, and the wide sky shaded from

turquoise blue to the deep blue of oncoming night.
Boys and girls ran back and forth across the wide
lawns, or clustered under the street lights. They
played harder, ran faster, shouted louder than usual,
for next Monday school would start.

The Miller girls and their father were still at the
supper table. Lou Emma had forgotten to put the
potatoes to cook in time and they had hard lumps in
them. The pork roast had gone into the oven too
soon, and it was dried out and the grease burned so
that the gravy tasted—*ook*. The gelatin dessert she
had worked so hard on didn't jell because she had
forgotten to put out the ice card and the ice melted.

"Never mind," her father said. "Tomorrow will
be better."

"It'll be worse," Maddy said. "We'll eat left-overs
from this."

Tears prickled inside of Lou Emma's nose.

"School's about to begin, girls. Wouldn't you like
to try a housekeeper? Some nice woman to relieve you
of all this work?"

"You promised, Papa," Lou Emma reminded him.

"No housekeepers," Maddy said. "Just us."

"All right. I only thought it might be easier on
you."

"Tomorrow I'll clean up the house till it shines,"
Maddy said.

"I'll give these left-overs to Vinnie for the chickens," Lou Emma said. "Tomorrow I'll cook real good. Cooking isn't hard. It's only remembering what to do when that's hard."

From the open door they heard Vinnie counting out for a game of Hide and Seek.

"We'll keep the *status quo*," Professor Miller smiled. "But tonight there's a full moon and I want you to go out and play with the others. I'll do the dishes."

Hide and Seek played by moonlight is a wild, scary game. They raced and ran through the pitchy black shadows, screaming and dodging whichever was It, trying to get Home Free.

Tommy came by, bringing Swish a kettle of watermelon rinds, the last of the season, and joined in the game. One by one the other boys and girls went home, but Tommy stayed on with the Wackers and the Millers. Mrs. Wacker called the Hiders and Seekers to the porch to rest a little. Lou Emma went after Swish, and he lay in the grass by the steps nibbling chunks of melon rind she tossed him. Now and then she took a nibble herself, noticing that the Biddles didn't eat their melon as close to the rind as the Millers did, and feeling a little superior.

Mr. Wacker sat smoking, the red eye of his cigar winking as he puffed on it. Miss Kate was in the wicker chair with Joy asleep on her lap. After Professor Miller finished the dishes he came and sat on the bottom step of the porch, his long legs in the yard by Swish. The girls lined up on the sagging cots, and Tommy and Hackberry perched on the porch rail. The old rocker groaned under Mrs. Wacker's weight.

The moon was high in the sky, its gold turned to pure silver.

"Harvest moon," Mrs. Wacker rocked heavily.

"Once out on the farm we had a moon like that when we got word the grasshoppers were comin' our way. We worked all night by moonlight to save the crops."

"Did you save 'em?" Maddy asked.

Mrs. Wacker sighed as if the memory even now was hard to endure. "There was no savin' anything from those devils. Our whole crop that year was one gallon of potatoes."

"How'd you get along?" Lou Emma asked, knowing the short span of meals covered by a gallon of potatoes.

"We had to take help. Gov'ment help. Railroad help. Help from Back East. It went against the grain, I can tell you, but it was that or starve. We ate so many rabbits that year I never wanted to see another 'un."

Tommy spoke up. "Ma says Kansas ought to put a gold rabbit atop the statehouse, like that codfish in Massachusetts that saved the settlers from starving. She claims she knew a man that ate so many rabbits his ears twitched backwards and forwards."

"Lavinia Biddle lived next farm to us," Mrs. Wacker explained to Miss Kate. "The man that twitched his ears was my cousin, Ez."

"Tell about Hiawatha and the moon," Lou Emma asked Miss Kate. "The part that tells what the shadows are."

Miss Kate shifted the sleeping Joy and recited as if the book were open before her:

> *And the good Nokomis answered,*
> *"Once a warrior, very angry,*
> *Seized his grandmother and threw her,*
> *Up into the sky at midnight.*
> *Right against the moon he threw her;*
> *'Tis her body that you see there."*

"A pretty hateful way to treat your grandmother," Maddy said.

"Aw, the moon's made outa green cheese," Hackberry said. "Those spots, they're mould. Mouldy old moon."

"I can recite *The Man in the Moon,* by James Whitcomb Riley," Eppie proffered, and did so, in spite of Hackberry's rude, buzzing noises.

"Listen to the child," Mrs. Wacker marveled. "She'll be on the stage yet."

With a shameful twinge of jealousy, Lou Emma thought that if Eppie, Vinnie, Hackberry, or even Joy, as much as sneezed, their mother thought it was the finest sneeze since Time began.

"Talkin' o' the spots on the moon," Mr. Wacker said. "I knew a feller that claimed he could predict weather by 'em. But he didn't do any better'n Jane here with her bunion."

"I'll put my bunion up against your rheumatism, any day," his wife said.

"What do you make o' those spots, Professor?" Mr. Wacker went on.

"They're mountains, valleys, craters, plains," Professor Miller said. "Back in the 1600's a man named Hevelius made a map of the moon that showed them. If we had a telescope I could show you," he said, and moved sharply as if the steps had become uncomfortable. Swish, at his feet, raised a small white head.

Professor Miller leaned forward and rubbed Swish's nose. "But I'd better stop talking about telescopes. They're far too expensive."

Maddy laughed, and Lou Emma was unhappily certain what her sister was about to say. "Lou Emma said we'd give the drill and make enough money to buy EKCC a telescope. Isn't that crazy? Nobody'd come."

"That will do, Maddy," Professor Miller said. "It was a generous thought, even if it was impractical. The telescope I want costs three hundred dollars. Dr. Biddle says that is completely out of the question."

Three hundred dollars? Lou Emma was shocked. Her father's whole salary . . . that he hadn't got yet . . . was eight hundred dollars.

"How're you going to get around it?" Mrs. Wacker asked.

"I'm not. I'm going to order a chart of the stars for three dollars and teach from that."

"Some rich man might give one," Maddy said. "Who's rich?"

"Mr. Garrett," Tommy answered promptly. "But you can't ask him this year. Pa's going to hit him up for a new grand piano for Rehearsal Hall."

Quiet descended on the porch, broken only by the groan of Mrs. Wacker's rocker. The moon sailed on, distant and silver.

"Why not make a telescope, Professor?" Miss Kate said.

"Land o' love, Kate," Mrs. Wacker protested.

Professor Miller looked up from scratching Swish's head. "Make a telescope? Make a telescope?"

"Papa can't drive a nail straight," Maddy said. "You should've seen the mess he got into back in Auden patching the roof."

"Papa can do lots of things," Lou Emma defended him. "Only, he didn't like patching the roof. He said he'd rather set out pans to catch the drips."

There was a laugh, and she wished she hadn't been so outspoken. Her father got up from the steps and stood in front of Miss Kate.

"What made you suggest that I could make a telescope?"

"Oh, I don't know." Then a quick change came in

her voice. "I do know, only I don't think I should say it."

"Please go on," Professor Miller said.

"Well, the way I got into the millinery business was by wanting a beautiful, beautiful hat that one of my married sisters had. I couldn't buy one, so I went to work and made one. And it was tacky. A *mess*. A bigger mess than your roof in Auden, I'm sure. But I learned from making it. And the next hat was a little better, and I kept trying." She stopped, then suddenly added, "So there."

Lou Emma waited, half-frightened, for her father to say scornfully that a hat was a foolish thing, and a telescope was an important scientific thing. But he didn't. He went on repeating: "Make a telescope? Make a telescope?"

"People don't make telescopes; they buy'em," Maddy said.

"Somebody has to make'em first," Lou Emma said.

"Galileo!" Professor Miller shouted so loudly that all of them jumped and Hackberry tumbled backward off the porch railing. "Galileo. I've told History classes a hundred times that he made his own telescope without even seeing one. Why didn't I think what I was saying?"

He turned and ran down the steps, stumbling over Swish, and falling full length in the yard. The astonished Swish bounded onto the porch, bleating loudly. Lou Emma started for her father, but he was on his feet.

"Sanguine Saturnini!" he roared, kicked the melon rind kettle, and raced across the yard into the small brown house next door. The bang of the door shattered the quiet of the night.

"Na-a-a-a-a," Swish complained, nuzzling Lou Emma. "Na-a-a-a-a."

"Land o' love, what'd the Professor say?" Mrs. Wacker gasped.

"We don't know," Maddy said. "He doesn't say it often, but when he does . . ." She left it unfinished.

"Do you know what it means, Miss Kate?" Lou Emma asked.

"I'd say it means that Eastern Kansas Classical College is going to have a telescope," Miss Kate said.

Chapter 15

The next morning, before breakfast, Professor Miller announced that he was going to the University of Kansas, at Lawrence, to consult Dr. Otto of the Science Department about making a telescope. He wouldn't even wait for the pancakes Lou Emma had made to carry out her resolution of last night to improve her cooking. She watched the Great Smith roar out of the yard as she poured the creamy batter onto the griddle. Just her luck that the pancakes were perfection and her father would never see nor taste them, she thought mournfully. But Maddy was exultant.

"A whole day to do exactly what we want to!"

"I thought you were going to clean up the house,"

said Lou Emma, feeling cranky. "You said so your very own self."

"That was before Papa got on a high horse about making a telescope. You know good'n' well he won't notice now if the dirt's an inch thick."

Lou Emma had to admit that her sister was right. She joined in recklessly. "Let's not wash the oatmeal pan, or make the beds, or even wash our teeth."

"Let's go back to bed with our clothes on and read all day," Maddy said.

For about a half-hour they lay back to back, Maddy reading the new *Youth's Companion,* Lou Emma the old, old copy of Charles Kingsley's *Water Babies* that she knew by heart. Then Maddy bounced out of bed.

"Let's do something else."

"For cat's sake!" Lou Emma wailed, her eyes still glued to the page, "you were the one that said let's stay in bed and read all day. I'm just good started."

"You've read that book a thousand times," Maddy said. "Let's go get a lunch up and go someplace and cook it."

Lou Emma hated to do what Maddy told her to, but the truth was she was already tired of lying in bed with her skirt band twisted around her waist and her feet tangled in the covers. Outdoors the weather was bright and blue and breezy. "All right. Let's go to the Chautauqua Grounds. Let's ask Vinnie and Eppie to go."

"It's no use," Maddy shrugged. "Mrs. Wacker's got 'em tied hand 'n' foot with hems to pick out and let down, clothes to iron, last year's books to find, all that stuff to get ready for school." She stretched luxuriously, reaching her fingers toward the low ceiling. "Are we lucky! The only girls in Gloriosa that can do what we want to all day long. No mother to tell us to pick out old hems and stuff."

Lou Emma rooted under the sheet for her slipper that was lost there. What would Maddy say if she told her it would be nice to have somebody notice that their skirts were cutting high water and the hems ought to be let down?

They had the Chautauqua Grounds to themselves, and once again Maddy gloried in their freedom. "Hurrah for Rule Number Three!" She turned a handspring.

"Aunt Jesse says that's no Rule. It's just organized laziness."

"Huh! Well, it's *our* organized laziness. It's not anybody else's."

They went to Assembly Hall, climbed to the platform, deserted and echoing to their footsteps, and "put on" some of the programs they remembered, applauding each other and giving the Chautauqua

Salute. Then they went down Lovers' Lane and built
a fire on the river's edge and cooked their food. The
potatoes, rolled in mud to bake, never did get done,
but the bacon and eggs were a big success. In the
late afternoon the weather changed and a growl of
thunder and a patter of rain startled them. They
started for home, Lou Emma with the skillet held
over her head for an umbrella. At the gateway of the
Chautauqua Grounds Maddy called back, "Let's go
to Miss Kate's shop till it lets up."

They were a bedraggled pair when they reached
the millinery shop, and Miss Kate laughed at their
appearance and made them take off their wet clothes
and sit back of the curtain, draped in odds and ends,
while their things dried. Rain kept the customers
away and it was fun to sit, snuggled on the old cot
and sip the hot tea Miss Kate made on the gas plate,
and listen to the stories she told of her life in Highbank. They shivered at the story of the Great Bliz-
zard when the Turner family burned all their corn

crop to keep from freezing. They laughed at her for saying she had helped her father quarry stone fence-posts.

It was still raining at closing time and they splashed home under Miss Kate's big black cotton umbrella. The girls begged her to stay with them "just till Papa gets home," and she agreed.

After supper they played three games of Parchesi. It was pitch black outside and the rain was pouring. Lou Emma plastered her nose against the window.

"Oughtn't Papa to be back now? How far is it to Lawrence?"

"Your father will be all right," Miss Kate said firmly. "Why don't you bring down those dark blue dresses and we'll let out the hems for school."

Maddy skipped upstairs and Lou Emma hunted scissors, pins, needles, and thread. Miss Kate brought some grosgrain ribbon out of her handbag and started making headbands with rosettes to match the red buttons on the dresses.

"I was going to surprise you with these, but this way I can measure and be sure they fit." She snipped off a length of ribbon. "Did I ever tell you girls that my Uncle Joshua was a water witch?"

One story led to another, and Lou Emma was surprised when the clock struck nine. She saw Miss Kate glance at the clock and at the black window but nothing showed in her face and voice and she tossed Maddy's headband to her with a smile.

"How about some popcorn?" she suggested.

But before Lou Emma could resurrect the old wire popper the Great Smith came snorting and hiccupping into the yard, the acetylene lamps dim in the rain. Into the kitchen came Professor Miller, mud from head to heels; he looked from one of the three to the other and sank with a relieved laugh into a chair by the kitchen table.

"Here I've been worrying about you girls for the past three hours and you've been snug as bugs in a rug. Kate, if that's potato soup on the stove I'll arrange for you to get a life-saving medal."

"It's potato soup," Miss Kate pushed the pan onto the range top and shook up the fire-box. "But I don't want a medal. I'd rather have a look through your telescope."

"Papa, where have you been?" Maddy demanded.

"We waited'n' waited'n' waited," Lou Emma said.

"Well, I've been in the ditch three times and stuck in the road four times, or was it the other way round? A man loses count. But before that I was talking with Dr. Otto and he thinks we can make a reflector telescope. They have a six-inch over there at K.U. He gave me a glass disk of porthole glass—that's so it will stand the pressure of grinding—and a couple of extra

disks to work with." He opened a newspaper-wrapped
package and put the three glass disks on the table. To
Lou Emma they were very unexciting, but she tried
to look pleased.

Miss Kate poured the hot potato soup into a bowl
and set out crackers.

"He lent me Draper's book on telescope-making,
too," Professor Miller began on the soup without
even stopping to wash his hands. "And he told me
about Foucault's formula for checking the grinding
of the concavity." Crunch went a handful of crackers
into the soup.

Maddy couldn't stand it. "Papa! You never let us
break crackers in our soup. And you always make us
wash our hands. What'll Miss Kate think?"

"Huh? Oh. Well, I apologize, Kate. I guess I did
get carried away. But the soup's so good and I was
so hungry—and so relieved that the girls were all
right."

"I think it's fine that you got things settled," Miss
Kate said. "And I'm glad you like the soup. But I'd
better be going now."

"Oh don't go," Professor Miller jumped up. "I
have a lot more to tell you. And I haven't really
thanked you yet."

"Some other time," Miss Kate shook out her still-
wet umbrella.

As she was telling the girls good-night, and starting out the door Professor Miller called after her. "By the way, Kate, one thing that held me up—I met a friend of yours in the ditch outside of town and I had to pull him out. A gasoline engine's better than a steam engine, you know. Especially for mud."

Laughing, Miss Kate hurried through the rain and the girls watched her until Wackers' door swallowed her up. Then they turned back to their father.

"Papa! You didn't!" Maddy's eyes were bright.

"Not Hardy Garrett?" Lou Emma crowed. "Not the Gentleman's Speedy Roadster?"

"The same," Professor Miller said. "And he was royally stuck."

"Why didn't you leave him there?" Maddy said, giggling.

"Till Spring, anyway," Lou Emma said.

"Girls!" Professor Miller said. "Where's your Christian charity? Besides, a lowly teacher could hardly leave the son of the chief benefactor of the college in a mudhole in the middle of Kansas. I must confess, I enjoyed my philanthropy."

He sent the girls to bed, urging them to get up early in the morning. He had a list of things to get together to start on the telescope and they left him reading it aloud and making notes: "Emery powder. Jeweler's rouge . . ."

"Papa's really on a high horse," Maddy said getting out of her dress.

"I'll never make pancakes as good," Lou Emma said, still regretting their brown perfection. "There goes Miss Kate's lamp out, now."

Maddy jumped into bed and turned away from the window. Lou Emma crawled in beside her. After a while Maddy said, "You awake?"

"A little," Lou Emma drowsed. "But not much. What d'you want?"

"Nothing, only . . . well, it was funny the way we said picking out hems and getting ready for school was such an awful job and we were lucky not to have to . . ."

You said it; I didn't, Lou Emma corrected silently.

". . . but when Miss Kate got us started it was kind of fun."

"Uh-huh," Lou Emma said.

A little more time went by and then Maddy said, "You know, I wouldn't mind Papa's getting married if it was Miss Kate. Would you?"

Lou Emma held her breath to keep down her happiness so that it wouldn't show in her voice and scare Maddy off.

"Uh-uh," was all she said, then she drifted into sleep to the sound of the rain on the roof overhead.

Chapter 16

September meant school in Gloriosa as it had in Auden. Lou Emma was thankful they had Vinnie and Eppie to go with and show them the important things such as which was the Girls' Side, and which was the Boys' Side, and how to keep the Music Teacher who came once a week from knowing she wasn't singing. She did better with the Art Teacher, who carried a sheaf of Perry Pictures by famous artists and told stories about them.

But Arithmetic was the same old bugbear. It was no surprise to have a note sent home to her father after the first test. School was so close to the small brown house that they came home for dinner at noon, walking with the Wackers—Hackberry a half-block ahead or behind.

At recess they found that their father's telescope had become the talk of the town. The teacher asked the Miller girls to tell the Fifth and Sixth Grade rooms about it. Lou Emma slid down in her desk and pretended to search for a pencil on the floor, but Maddy gave a complete report. So complete that she finally had to be told to be seated.

"You're the rage, Papa," Maddy told him at noon. "Everybody's talking about your telescope."

"I wish you'd stop calling it 'my telescope.' It belongs to EKCC in general and the Astronomy classes in particular."

"You ought to get credit," Maddy insisted. "You started it."

"Teachers should not care about credit. They should care about their students. And my students are learning—along with me. Even if we're not sure whether this telescope is going to be a success or not."

"Great Granny! If you don't know if it'll work, why don't you quit?"

Professor Miller shut Draper's book on telescope-making with a snap. "And lose the fun of learning? No Maddy, I strongly believe in the right to experiment."

"Is the 'right to experiment' for me 'n' Lou Emma, too?"

With a groan her father shook his head. "Parents

talk too much. Now you'll jump off the college bel-fry and say I told you it was right to experiment."

"*Uh*uh," Maddy said, "I already jumped out the hayloft in Auden."

"And *I* got a broken collarbone," Lou Emma said.

"I'm afraid that often happens to innocent by-standers. Lou Emma, please look on the list and see who's coming to work on the grinding tonight."

The list hung by the kitchen door. "Georgetta Kettlewell and Eugene Martin from the Astronomy class. Dr. Biddle when he can get away from the Board of Stewards meeting at the church. And Mr. Wacker."

"Eugene's the one that took three cups of cocoa last time," Maddy reminded Lou Emma. "You'd better make extra."

Professor Miller frowned. "I'm not at all sure Dr. Otto at K.U. would approve of this cocoa business. It doesn't seem scientific to me."

"Why, it's the very best part," Lou Emma said, "Everybody says so."

The morning after Professor Miller's trip to Law-rence, Maddy had gone over to Wackers' very early in the morning, refusing to tell anyone why she went. She returned in triumph with a small red felt straw-berry that Miss Kate used to sharpen her sewing needles. "There's emery powder in it," she said. "You said you needed emery powder to start the telescope and there it is. I asked Miss Kate for it."

Their father had praised Maddy so much for her cleverness in remembering he had needed emery powder, and knowing that the felt strawberry contained it, that Lou Emma felt stupid and left out by comparison. Only when he listed the other things needed and included "one prism" did she take heart. At least she knew where a *prism* was. She went to Vinnie and offered to trade her button charm string, her new book satchel, and the grosgrain ribbon headband Miss Kate had made for her for the prism. Reluctantly, Vinnie traded, cautioning Lou Emma not to let Mrs. Wacker know where the prism had come from.

But when she brought it to her father, complete with its nest of white feathers, he had told her gently that the prism needed for the telescope was different from the kind Carry Nation knocked off the lamp in the saloon. He suggested that Lou Emma save the Carry Nation prism for History because it belonged there, but the harder he tried to explain that her offer was as good as Maddy's gift the worse she felt.

Miss Kate caught her moping in the barn, wiping tears on Swish's back. The story came out and Miss Kate nodded, supplying a fresh handkerchief.

"No wonder you felt bad. Let me see that prism you're talking about."

Lou Emma brought it from the old feed bin where it was hidden. As she held it up to the light rainbow colors danced on Swish's back. She forgot to cry.

"Beautiful!" Miss Kate said and touched the prism so that the colors bounced over the barn. "Did you know that it's just ordinary sunlight that goes through the prism and turns into a rainbow? That's what we'll do, Lou Emma, we'll find your prism."

"I guess I don't know what you mean."

"We'll find some ordinary thing you do that can turn into a rainbow."

"I can't sing, I can't work arithmetic, I can't climb trees . . ."

"Stop it!" Miss Kate said. "Tell me what you can do."

"Not much. Maddy's the smart one. I can cook— a little."

"Cooking will be fine. We'll have cooking in this telescope before you can say Andromeda Major."

"Whatever's that?"

"I think it's a bunch of stars, but don't tell your father. It might turn out to be an officer in the Roman Army."

In the meantime work on the telescope had begun.

To make a reflector telescope the first thing is to make a main mirror to do the reflecting. That had to be ground by hand from the glass disk . . . the one made of porthole glass that Dr. Otto had given Professor Miller. It was thick, flat, round, and rough on the edges. These were stroked smooth with a carborundum stone borrowed from Mr. Wacker, who borrowed it from the Santa Fe railroad.

Now the disk, from this time called the *glass blank,* was placed on the head of a barrel between four cleats to hold it steady. The barrel was partly filled with gravel so that it wouldn't move.

All this apparatus had been put in the Millers' front room because the natural light was better there and the base burner could be regulated to hold the temperature to an even 68 degrees.

First came the rough grinding. The glass blank was covered with a mixture of emery powder and water called "slurry." Maddy's little strawberry-ful was in the first mixture. Then, one of the plate-glass disks, smaller than the glass blank, was rubbed over it. This smaller disk was called the *tool disk.* The rubbing was kind of like a dance—a minuet, maybe. Back and forth for ten strokes, rotate the glass blank a fraction of a turn, take three steps around the side of the barrel. Repeat. Back and forth, back and forth, around and around the barrel. In time this grinding would wear a concave place in the glass blank. The tool disk, at the same time, would become convex.

"Concave? Convex?" Lou Emma puzzled.

"Simple as a spoon." Her father tapped the bowl of a kitchen spoon. "Concave." He turned it over and tapped the back. "Convex."

But the rest of it wasn't that easy to understand. Lou Emma tried hard.

When they finished grinding out the main mirror from the glass blank, her father explained, it would be placed at one end of a tube. The other end would be open. The light from the object they wanted to see—the moon, for instance—would come in the open end of the tube, be reflected from the main mirror, and since that was concave, it would *bend* the light and send it back up the tube.

"Do you understand so far?" he asked. She shook her head unhappily.

"Well, try—try—now, at a point three-fourths of the way back up the tube we place the prism. And the prism *bends* the light and sends it through the eyepiece that comes through the side of the tube. So— what do we see through the eyepiece, Lou Emma?"

A long silence. "I don't have any idea, Papa."

"*The moon,* Lou Emma. Now—listen carefully. The main mirror . . ."

He went over it again and again, but she never did

understand what happened to the light, how it could be bent, and especially how the light from the moon knew it was supposed to go into the EKCC telescope and do all that bending. It seemed simpler to go outdoors and look at the moon in the sky. And a *lot* more fun.

At last she gave up trying to understand, and tried only to keep out of the way. But even that wasn't easy. Every evening the house was crowded with members of the Astronomy classes, the Physics classes that had joined in, the Congregational minister, Dr. Biddle, Mr. Garrett, Mr. Wacker, and a dozen others.

When they overflowed the front room into the kitchen, Lou Emma walked out. The screech of the slurry between the glass blank and the tool disk followed her. She could hear her father instructing a new grinder: "Spread the slurry, sprinkle water from your fingertips, put your full weight on the tool disk. Harder . . . harder . . . Back and forth, back and forth, ten strokes, rotate the glass blank . . . again, again."

She hurried away to get out of hearing and went over to Wackers'. No one was at home but Miss Kate, who was trimming a hat with red ribbon.

"I'm glad you came," she snipped a loop of thread. "I have an idea about that prism we're looking for, for you."

"I don't want it any more," Lou Emma said. "I hate that old telescope."

"Do you hate the telescope? Or do you hate being left out?"

Lou Emma sat and sulked. For two cents, for *one* cent, she'd leave.

Miss Kate hummed and threaded her needle anew. At last Lou Emma spoke.

"What kind of idea?"

"The Professor is worried at the cost of an eyepiece for the telescope."

"Why don't you call him Cyrus? He calls you Kate."

"Don't change the subject." Miss Kate's face was pink. Or was it the red ribbon she was stitching, reflected?

"I heard him say the eyepiece would cost fifteen dollars," Lou Emma admitted, "and he hated to ask Dr. Biddle to buy it since the college hadn't paid salaries yet. But I don't see what that's got to do with me."

"Well, I've been watching those people streaming into your house. They stay for hours. Most of them eat supper about six, or earlier. By nine they're hungry."

"They can starve for all I care," Lou Emma said gloomily.

Miss Kate ignored her. "If you came in at nine

carrying a tray with cups of hot cocoa and offered it
at five cents a cup, I think it would sell. And you
could put the profit you'd make on the cost of the
eyepiece for the telescope."

"Why—that's wonderful!" Lou Emma said. "And
have whipped cream and spice cake and . . ."

"Hold on," Miss Kate said. "You're running out of
profit already. If a box of cocoa costs ten cents, a
pound of sugar costs five cents, a gallon of milk costs
fifteen cents, how much profit is there in selling cocoa
at five cents a cup?"

"How many cups in a gallon?"

"That's for you to figure out." Miss Kate handed
her a pencil.

Lou Emma looked suspicious. "Is this a scheme to
get me to do arithmetic?"

"Goodness no. It just happens that in any kind of
business you have to know profit and loss. And I
think Mrs. Wacker would sell you milk at 12% discount."

"Discount!" Lou Emma screeched. "That horrible
stuff!"

"The discounts I get on hat findings from the
wholesale houses can make the difference in profit
and loss for Miss Kate's Chapeaux."

Lou Emma started to protest further but instead
she took the pencil and began to figure. Presently she

looked up, pleased. "It would cost twenty-seven and an eighth cents per gallon to make the cocoa. Sixteen cups in a gallon. I could sell it for eighty cents and make fifty-two and seven eighths cents profit."

"And you told me you couldn't do arithmetic!"

Lou Emma pondered. "It's different if it's real."

"I think you can figure a little closer. Your sixteen cups are measuring cups and that's more than the average serving. I'd say eighteen cups."

"Hurrah! More profit." Lou Emma took up her pencil.

"There'll be times when you won't sell it all," Miss Kate cautioned.

"Then we'll drink it for breakfast," Lou Emma said.

"Why, you're a regular Hetty Green." Miss Kate looked at the clock. "Eight-fifteen. If we hustle we can have the cocoa ready by nine."

"Right now? Tonight?"

"No time like the present."

Lou Emma's old shyness crept upon her. "Maybe I ought to ask Papa."

"Didn't I hear something about the 'right to experiment?'" Lou Emma nodded. "This is an experiment, that's all. Here's a recipe for cocoa I cut out of the *Ladies' Home Journal.* And here's something else."

It was a hand-lettered sign on white cardboard. Pink velvet ribbon framed it and tiny blue forget-me-nots decorated it. In fancy script it announced:

Miss Miller's Refreshments
Starlight Cocoa. Five Cents
Per Delicious Cup. All Profits
To ERCC Telescope Eyepiece.

The kitchen at the Miller house was empty. The screech-scratch of the slurry on the glass blank could be heard over the murmur of voices in the front room.

Lou Emma got out a big pot to make the cocoa, a saucepan for the syrup, and measured milk, sugar, water, and cocoa as the recipe directed. She added the dash of salt recommended and got down the vanilla extract.

Miss Kate sniffed the vanilla smell. "I always remember a boy I used to go with in Highbank that put vanilla on for hair tonic. He was some punkins!"

"Why didn't you ever . . ." Lou Emma began, then faltered.

"Why didn't I ever get married?"

"I'm sorry. Aunt Jesse said it was very indelicate to ask and that an unmarried female should always say her condition was one of her own choice."

"'Unmarried female . . . condition . . . indelicate . . .'" Miss Kate sputtered. "That's quite a statement. Well, mine is simpler. I'm not married because I never loved anyone who asked me. My mother says I'm too choosy. My married sisters say there's not that much difference in men. I only know I'd have to love and respect a man."

Lou Emma said, "I wish that Papa . . ."

"Stir the milk," Miss Kate interrupted. "Nothing's worse than scorched milk."

"Yes ma'am," Lou Emma stirred up a whirlpool in the hot milk. For the second time that evening she noticed that Miss Kate's face was pink.

The cocoa was poured into cups set on a big tin tray. Taste-testing from the tip of a spoon Lou Emma decided it was good. *Really* good. Miss Kate hung the fancy sign around Lou Emma's neck and handed her the tray, adding to it a china bowl with three nickels in it. "That's to make change. Now, go ahead."

Panic choked in Lou Emma's throat. "Aren't you going with me?"

"Certainly not. This is your prism." Miss Kate steered her through the open door. "Smile, Lou Emma. Molasses catches more nickels than vinegar."

The front room could not have held more than a dozen people with all the apparatus, but to Lou Emma it seemed at least a hundred eyes stared at her.

Why did I ever do such a silly thing?

Her father frowned. Maddy put her hand to her mouth.

"Best idea yet!" It was Mr. Garrett. "Starlight cocoa? Let me buy the first cup." A nickel clinked into the bowl.

"Thank you," she said hoarsely.

"Splendid. Capital." Dr. Biddle took a cup. "Delicious, too."

Tommy popped up from nowhere. "Hey, Pa, get one for me."

"Lemme stop grinding, Professor," a lanky student begged. "Cocoa's my favorite fruit."

"Isn't he a *case?*" a blonde girl giggled. "A cup for me, please."

The tray felt lighter and lighter. Suddenly the last cup was lifted. Lou Emma went back to the kitchen, the china bowl jingling with nickels. "It worked, Miss Kate! Just the way you said it would!"

But Miss Kate had gone. On the mirror over the sink she had written with a bar of soap, "Good Luck!" Under the words was drawn a lop-sided prism.

Autumn was gold and red, then brown and gray. It was half-past October.

Starlight Cocoa became more and more popular as

work on the telescope went along. Some evenings
Lou Emma had to make extra, and she learned to
halve or quarter her recipe, and to juggle fractions as
she put down her expenses in the little notebook
Miss Kate had given her.

The rough grinding on the glass blank was done,
and the fine grinding started. To do this Professor
Miller and Mr. Wacker made a new tool. Its surface
was covered with pitch—borrowed from the Santa Fe
—and embedded in the pitch was a much finer grade
of emery powder. Fine grinding had to be done more
carefully and the results measured with hair-splitting
accuracy. Every item used had to be cleaned after
each change in the grade of emery power. The base
burner was kept burning low lest the glass blank
get chilled.

"It might break if it gets too cold, or too hot, or it
might break when we start the silvering," Professor
Miller said to the girls.

"What would you do if it broke?" Lou Emma
asked in a hushed tone.

"Shoot myself," he said, then he laughed at her
shocked face. "Why, I suppose I'd do what Brashears
did when his first mirror broke in the silvering. His
wife set out the grinding tools the next night and he
started all over again. I don't have a wife but I have
two good girls."

"We're not really good," Lou Emma said. "But we love you."

"That's enough for me," he said. "Let's walk over to Wackers' and see how Hack's getting along with the tube for the telescope."

They found Mr. and Mrs. Wacker and Miss Kate in the kitchen, talking about the telescope.

"To see the moon an' the stars," Mrs. Wacker marveled. "Oh, it was a lucky day for EKCC when you came here, Professor."

Miss Kate glanced up from the ostrich plumes she was curling. "It will be even luckier when he writes his textbook on early Roman history."

"Textbook? Early Roman history?" Professor Miller snorted. "Where did you get the crazy, idiotic, foolish idea that I am planning to write a textbook?"

"Oh," Miss Kate smiled at the plume, "you told me how our way of life had come from so many Roman ideas, and that no textbook you had ever used treated the subject the way it should. I suppose that's how I got the crazy, foolish, idiotic idea you could write a better one."

"Sure he could," Maddy said. "He said last night the textbook he has now is a botched-up job."

"And you gave the last one you used in Auden to the trash man," Lou Emma said. "Do it, Papa."

"See here," Professor Miller smacked the table.

"Just because you talked me into that goat, Kate Turner . . ."

"Me? I? Swish?"

"And just because you got me into this telescope business . . ."

"I never in the wide world . . ."

"You are not pushing me into writing a bad text-book on Roman history."

"It wouldn't be bad; it would be good," Miss Kate said softly.

Lou Emma pulled his arm. "Papa, when you talk about Roman history you make me feel as if it was all true and it was only last week it happened. 'Hannibal at the gates,' and Cato with his red hair, like Hackberry's, and Cornelia and 'these are my jewels,' and all."

"My dear, other men have written those stories far better than I could. It would take me years. I might even have to go to Rome. Why, I have no right to discuss such a thing."

"You believe in 'the right to experiment,' " Lou Emma reminded him.

"Not with History," Professor Miller said firmly. "That is different. Why, I've taught History for years."

"Exactly." Miss Kate spoke to the ostrich plume. "Exactly."

The silence that followed was explosive. Lou Emma held her breath. Professor Miller stalked out of the room. The door slammed behind him.

"Women!" Mr. Wacker said. "Always pushin' men around."

Mrs. Wacker spun toward him, her red hair fairly crackling. "I'd like to know when any woman ever pushed you around, Hack Wacker. Tell me just one time."

Lou Emma and Maddy tiptoed to the door, turning in time to get Miss Kate's signal of her finger to her lips.

The next morning nothing was said about the scene at the Wackers'. Professor Miller ate his oatmeal hurriedly, and spoke only to say that they would soon be ready for the eyepiece of the telescope. After he left, Lou Emma poured out her money and counted it. $10.60, and every cent profit. She had been careful with her bookkeeping. She enjoyed setting sums down in the little lines in the notebook. There had been some losses. Twice she had scorched the milk . . . ugh . . . and had to pour it out and start over. One awful evening she had spilled the whole gallon of cocoa and mopped for what seemed like days to clean it up. But now that Starlight Cocoa was a part of the experiment, the students in the

Astronomy classes would come out to the kitchen and sit around the table, talking about their work. From them she caught a glimmer of what was going on.

"I don't mean I understand it," she explained to Miss Kate. "But I kind of see why they like it. Stars, comets, planets, so far away, so *trillionally far*. It stretches my head to think about it."

"Tell me about it," Miss Kate went on with her work in the back of the millinery shop but she seemed to give Lou Emma all her attention.

"Well, Mars has two moons. Deimos and Phobos. And Sirius, that's the Dog Star, is the brightest star. And I like the names—Orion, Arcturus, Aldebaran. And the Pleiades—that's the Seven Sisters, only one, Merope, is lost half the time."

"I think that's remarkable," Miss Kate fitted rosy velvet around a buckram crown, took it off and re-fitted it. "How's your arithmetic?"

"I'm doing better," Lou Emma said, surprised. "Why'd you ask?"

"Just a wild guess." Miss Kate began to stitch the velvet.

"What you said to Papa about the textbook," Lou Emma began. "He had H-O-G out last night. First time since he got on his high horse about the tele-scope. Maddy and I found it when we changed sheets this morning. And there were lots of notes stuck between the pages and the top one was, 'Ideas for Text-books.' Do you think . . ."

"It's not our time to think. It's our time to keep mum."

At that moment Maddy stomped in, her lip stuck out and her dark blue eyes stormy. "D'you know what Adelaide Moss said?"

"I don't want to know if it makes you look like that," Miss Kate said.

"She said Papa would never in this world or the next get that silly telescope to work, and that looking at the moon wasn't what he was paid for at the college. Furthermore she said . . ." Maddy took a deep breath. "She said five cents was too much for a cup of cocoa."

Lou Emma jumped from the cot. "Too much? Why it's barely enough. I have hardly any profit the way it is and if milk goes up . . ."

"That's not all," Maddy went on.

Miss Kate cut more velvet for the brim of the hat. "If you're determined to tell what Adelaide said, be sure it's exactly the way she said it."

"So help me Hannah, on a stack of Bibles a mile high," Maddy lifted her right hand. "She said Lou Emma oughtn't be allowed to sell cocoa at such an outlandish price, and it was prob'ly made out of skim milk and watered at that. And she's going to sell cocoa outside our house with whipped cream on top, *two* cups for a nickel."

"She can't do it. I won't let her," Lou Emma twisted her hands.

"Calm down," Miss Kate said. "In the first place Adelaide won't do all that hard work. In the second place you know by your own bookkeeping that she'd be out of business in a jiffy, if she did."

Maddy said, "In the third place she won't be doing anything until her nose stops bleeding."

"You didn't?" Lou Emma didn't know whether to be horrified or happy.

"I did so, and I wish she had two noses so I could bloody both of'em."

"It sounds to me as if Adelaide got what she asked for," Miss Kate said.

But Lou Emma was not easily comforted. Adelaide had a mother to take up for her; the Miller girls had only their father and he was no match for an angry female. "Why'd you do it?" she mourned to Maddy. "Now when Mrs. Moss comes steamin' to Papa he'll get a housekeeper for sure and certain to look after us better."

They went by the Big Dollar to buy a box of cocoa, and then to the post-office to get the mail. Maddy shuffled through it.

"Book advertisements . . . book advertisements . . . book . . . book . . . book . . . Rats! Nothing but book advertisements for Papa. He's got too many books now."

"Wait, I think one of those . . ." Lou Emma looked over Maddy's shoulder but Maddy stuffed the envelopes into her coat pocket.

"Don't be such a fuss-budget," Maddy said. "And I thought you'd thank me for pushing Adelaide in the snoot. I did it for you."

"Thanks," Lou Emma said. "Only . . . well, thanks, anyway."

"Hmph!" Maddy sniffed and walked away.

"Don't be mad," Lou Emma hurried after her. "And look at the letters again. I'm almost sure there's one from Aunt Jesse in among the book advertisements."

It turned out that Lou Emma was right. Miss Jesse Miller's fine copperplate hand-writing was unmistakable. The letter was addressed to Professor Miller. Cross at being caught in a mistake, Maddy thrust the letter at Lou Emma.

"If you're so smart then you can carry it."

"But Maddy, I only . . ." Lou Emma had to hurry to catch up. Maddy's head was turned haughtily aside. Quietly, Lou Emma slipped Aunt Jesse's letter into Maddy's coat pocket with the others.

They walked on through the October dusk. The smell of burning leaves hung over the town. Maddy suddenly halted.

"It's The Creepers . . . and they're *against* us."

"Oh nooooo," Lou Emma moaned.

"Through the alley!" Maddy began to run, Lou Emma at her heels. The alley dead-ended and they had to climb a fence and landed in a chicken-yard. Chickens scuttered and squawked and a man shouted angrily. A dog ran at them.

The Miller girls crashed through a gate, ran across the street, through another yard, and into a vegetable garden where they floundered through frosted-down tomato vines. Still the dog pursued them, barking noisily. They crouched beside a rain barrel at the edge of a house. The dog came racing up.

"Git!" Lou Emma commanded him. "Git for home!"

"The Creepers! They're coming!" Maddy grabbed Lou Emma's arm.

"Run for your life!"

They tore past an astonished old lady coming out with a kettle to dip rain-water from the barrel. The dog ran with them, delighted with the chase.

Ahead in the dusk Lou Emma saw the tall arches of the bridge over the river. She veered in that direction, her throat aching for breath. Maddy passed her and climbed on the bridge railing. The dog leaped excitedly at Maddy's ankles.

"Get away!" she screamed, "Get away!"

The dog leaped higher. Lou Emma threw a clod at him, as she hurried to Maddy's side. Suddenly Maddy jerked off her coat, and using it as a weapon, shook it in the dog's face. He backed away. Taking her coat by the hem, Maddy shook it violently and the dog tucked his tail between his legs and ran for home.

"See!" Maddy said in triumph. "See!"

"The letters," Lou Emma panted. "The letters . . . they went over the side . . . I saw'em go. Look."

She pointed down at the dark water where for a few moments the letters floated like strange white fish before they disappeared.

"Oh well," Maddy said. "Nothing but book advertisements. Papa won't really care, will he?"

"Maddy," Lou Emma said in a curious, choked voice. "Maddy—the letter from Aunt Jesse was in with the others. I put it in your pocket when you weren't looking."

Chapter 17

Tommy Biddle's Hallowe'en party for the Methodist Sunday School classes was the big event of the season. It was a masquerade party, and no one could come without a mask.

"We'll take 'em off before refreshments," Tommy promised when he came to deliver the witch's-hat-shaped invitations. "Nobody can eat good through those little bitty mask mouths."

"What's refreshments going to be?" Hackberry asked.

"Don't know yet. Hilda's sore at me. I put some high-life on her German beau's horse and he ran for a half-mile like a real champ. He calls her *mein schatzi.*"

"A horse can talk German?" Maddy asked.

"Naw, her *dumkopf* beau calls Hilda that. Well, I've got to be on my way." He looked at the invitations. "Mosses, Strunks, Ellises, McCords."

Lou Emma, Maddy, Vinnie, and Eppie decided that they would keep their costumes secret from everybody else. "We'll know. Us four an' no more," Vinnie said.

But Mrs. Wacker put a stop to that. Hackberry had to be included.

"I don't wanna go," Hackberry sulked. "Not in no crazy get-up."

"He's got to go," Eppie told the others. "Mama's not going to let us go unless he goes. She says it's time he got civilized and she's starting now."

"Let's ask Miss Kate how to bring him 'round," Maddy said.

When Miss Kate suggested that he go as Blackbeard the Pirate, Hackberry forgot his complaints and spent hours working on a murderous tin cutlass. Vinnie made a beard of black yarn, and he slept in it for a week, "to get my face used to it."

Eppie and Vinnie were going as *Helen's Babies,* the title of a popular novel among the grownups. Their costumes were long white nightgowns, pink crepe paper baby bonnets, nursing bottles, and celluloid rattles borrowed from Joy.

"But what are *we* going to wear?" Maddy asked Lou Emma for the tenth time.

"I thought Papa could think up some Greek or Roman costume, but he's too busy with the telescope. They're down to polishing the main mirror with jeweler's rouge, and there's reddish brown spots of it on the sofa, like hives."

"They're getting ready to silver the mirror," Maddy said. "Papa told me when he went to get the silver nitrate crystals. They're poison as poison. Mr. Ellis sent along some distilled water for him to use, too."

"Oh Maddy, I hope it works," Lou Emma said.

Maddy lowered her voice. "Every time I make up Papa's bed now there's a whole slug of notes on the floor. The top one says, 'First Look At Roman History.' He's really writing that textbook."

"First Look at Roman History by Cyrus Harper Miller," Lou Emma said reverently. "Just think, there'll be book advertisements of that."

Maddy laughed. "Don't forget that Miss Kate put him up to writing it. D'you s'pose she could get him to fix the leg on the kitchen stove?"

"Nope," Lou Emma said. "Papa really wants to write a textbook, the same as he really wanted to make a telescope . . . even if he didn't know it. But he doesn't care a snap about fixing stove legs."

"Oh well . . ." Maddy shrugged. "But what are we going to wear to the party? I thought I'd be a lady pirate but Hackberry raved and caved till I gave up. What do you want to be?"

"I don't know." Lou Emma crossed her fingers. She knew very well what she wanted to be. Titania, Queen of the Fairies. Like the one in *A Midsummer Night's Dream* at Chautauqua. But to say she wanted to be a queen sounded terribly stuck-up.

"We could be devils," Maddy's eyes sparkled. "With horns and tails and pitchforks. And dye Papa's union suits red for devil-suits."

"At a Sunday School party?"

"Devils are in the Bible. They talk about them at Sunday School."

"I don't think Mrs. Biddle would like it. Anyway, Papa's union suits are so worn and patched no respectable devil would wear'em."

After school they met at Miss Kate's Chapeaux to consider the problem of their costumes. "Pirates are out, devils are out, babies are out, witches and ghosts are a dime a dozen," Maddy said disconsolately. "I want something special. Something that's just for *me*."

Miss Kate took a book from the ironing-board where it was propped open. It was Mrs. Wacker's Chautauqua copy of American Poets. She read aloud:

With him dwelt his dark-eyed daughter
Wayward as the Minnehaha,
With her moods of shade and sunshine,
Eyes that smiled and frowned alternate,
Feet as rapid as the river,
Tresses flowing like the water . . .

She looked up from the book at Lou Emma. "It's a perfect description of Maddy. Mr. Longfellow must have had her in mind."

"It's perfect," Lou Emma echoed. "Perfect as plum pie."

"Oh Miss Kate," Maddy's face glowed. "Tell me what to do and I'll be the best Minnehaha that Gloriosa, Kansas, ever saw."

"Start by reading the poem," Miss Kate handed her the book. "I have feathers, beads, and some chamois for buckskin. And I do believe I have some old moccasins that my father got from an Indian trader."

"What will Lou Emma be? She's too blonde for an Indian!"

What would Miss Kate say? Lou Emma waited, half-scared. A cook in a white cap and apron? A Sunbonnet girl with a scrub-brush?

"Titania, Queen of the Fairies is exactly right for Lou Emma. Remember how she looked at Chautauqua?"

Her dress was of white tarlatan with silver stars scattered between the layers of the skirt. Her high-peaked crown was silver and so was her star-tipped wand. She had wings of gauze, wired to stand out, and embroidered with silver bugle beads so that they looked as if they had been dipped in frost. The dress had *no sleeves*. Instead it had straps across the shoulders.

The morning of the party Miss Kate rolled Lou Emma's hair up in kid curlers. All day long it pulled, pinched, and worried her. But in the evening when Miss Kate took down the curlers and brushed her hair into soft golden curls that lay about her bare shoulders, she knew it was worth it.

Looking at herself in the mirror, Lou Emma suddenly wished that her mother could see her. Maddy came over to share the mirror. Her dark braids shone from brushing. They were held back by a beaded headband from which a long pheasant feather nodded. The fringed chamois skirt and shirt were just right.

"I hate to put on my mask," Lou Emma adjusted her white satin domino. "Will all my curls be gone by tomorrow, Miss Kate?"

"If they are we'll put them up again. And I'll show you how."

Lou Emma gave her a hug, careful not to crush

her tarlatan skirt, even in her gratitude. "Thank you a million times."

"Three million times," Maddy added her hug. Then together the Miller girls floated downstairs.

The telescope workers had already gathered, but they stopped to admire the girls. Lou Emma reassured them that Miss Kate was going to serve Starlight Cocoa for her, "just this once." With old-fashioned courtesy, Mr. Garrett gave Lou Emma his arm. Dr. Biddle bowed to Maddy and escorted her to the Great Smith, waiting at the door.

They had to wait for the Wackers, and Professor Miller looked at his daughters. "What Kate Turner hath wrought! You'll be the prettiest pair at the party."

"Please don't say 'Pretty is as pretty does,' the way Aunt Jesse does," Maddy said.

Her father tweaked one of her braids. "I wish you girls wouldn't be so hard on Jesse. She means well."

"Means well" covers all the things that go wrong, Lou Emma thought. *Like those crocheted caps. And Miss Jenkins, and the rest. And saying we mustn't talk about our mother to Papa.*

But she said nothing. Tonight she was Titania, Queen of the Fairies.

The big house on Eclectic Avenue was dark and spooky. Candles wavered in grinning Jack-o-lanterns.

Party guests were sent to the outside cellar door where they came up steep, cobwebby steps. At the head of the stairs, a grinning skull on a table was lighted by a lone candle. A hand thrust at them from behind a dark curtain.

"Greetings," came in graveyard tones. "Shake the hand of one Gone Before."

Shrieking, pulling back, but at last taking the hand, the Millers and the Wackers clutched a glove dipped in ice water.

"Pass on," said the voice.

Jumpy and excited, they came to the kitchen where masked, costumed figures bobbed for apples around a washtub. Lou Emma wouldn't trust her curls to a possible drenching. She went to the front parlor, where a tent had been made by draping blankets over the grand piano. A sign was over the opening:

MADAM SEEZALL KNOWZALL, GYPSY FORTUNE TELLER.

A long line of witches, ghosts, Spanish dancers and Southern Belles waited their turn. In the back parlor a row of masqueraders chewed at yards of string to get to a marshmallow in the middle.

A cowboy with a western hat, red neckerchief, a curly moustache, and woolly chaps circled Lou Emma. His mask slipped and she thought she saw freckles on his eyelids, but he fixed the mask before she could be sure.

"Boys and girls!" Mrs. Biddle clapped her hands. "We'll have some games."

"*Post Office!*" yelled a fat clown and hid back of a chair.

Mrs. Biddle ignored him. "Our first game is Clap In and Clap Out. Instead of our real names we will use the characters we represent." She seized on Hackberry. "Now who is this jolly sailor lad?"

"I'm a PIRATE," yelled Hackberry. "I'M BLACKBEARD. And I'll never come to another silly party long as I live." He stomped from the room.

"Mama shouldn't've tried to civilize him," Eppie said.

A girl in an elegant pink satin crinoline-puffed skirt with her hair powdered white announced, "I'm Martha Washington, wife of our First President."

"Splendid," Mrs. Biddle said. "I'm sure you know the rules. Boys in the front parlor, girls in the dining-room. I'll be the doorkeeper."

As the groups separated, Martha Washington waved her fan at the boys. "Ta-ta," she called.

"I hope the wife of the First President never acted that way," Maddy said.

"It's Adelaide," Lou Emma said. "Those slippers are her summer whites painted."

"Next," called the fortune teller. Lou Emma crawled into the tent beneath the piano. Madam Seezall Knowzall looked very much like Miss Lawrence of the EKCC Fine Arts faculty. She had an upside-down fish bowl for a crystal ball and a Dream Book. By the light of a candle she examined Lou Emma's palm.

"A dark woman is coming into your life," she said. "Next."

A dark woman? Could it be Miss Kate with her dark hair and her dark eyes? Lou Emma longed to ask, but already Maddy was crawling into the tent. She backed out and straightened her tarlatan skirt. It must be Miss Kate. It *must* be.

Clap In and Clap Out was in full swing. Mrs. Biddle hurried the game along. Then they had a game of Musical Chairs. Madam Seezall Knowzall came out from her tent to play the piano and Lou Emma was sure that she was Miss Lawrence. Still, her words lingered. *A dark woman.*

At last Mrs. Biddle announced the Grand March where First Prize for the costumes would be given. One to the boys, one to the girls. They lined up, the boys jeering and shoving, the girls nervous and intent. Mrs. Biddle, Mr. Christy, Superintendent of the Sunday School, and Mrs. Mauldin from next door were the judges. As Miss Lawrence played marches

they went around and around the big rooms. Mr.
Christy held up his hand: "First Prize for the boys—
BLACKBEARD."

There were shouts and applause, but Hackberry
hung back, and Tommy and J.T. had to drag him
up to get the prize, a box of orange and black taffy.

"First Prize for the girls . . ." Mr. Christy began,
but Mrs. Mauldin shook her head. Mrs. Biddle mo-
tioned for Miss Lawrence to play more marches. The
girls paraded, trying to hear what the judges were
saying.

"LouEmmaLouEmmaLouEmma," Vinnie mum-
bled as if she recited a charm.

"Adelaide's the best," a new girl said. "Her costume cost $3.86 for the material alone."

"And a dressmaker made it," a Southern Belle said.

"Miss Kate Turner made Lou Emma's," Maddy
said, confident of the reputation of Miss Kate's
Chapeaux.

"She made it free," Adelaide said. "My mother
paid for mine."

"Now girls," Mr. Christy said, "All your costumes
are so good that we've decided to give two prizes.
First Prize to Titania, Queen of the Fairies. Second
Prize to Martha Washington. Step forward, please."

It was as if Lou Emma had picked up a giant prism
and looked at the party through it. Her prize was the

same as Hackberry's, but it might have been gold and jewels. As she took the box of taffy from Mr. Christy's hand, Martha Washington bumped into her. The box flew into the middle of the room and instantly the candy was scattered among the milling boys.

"Excuse *me*," Martha Washington said, without regret.

It wasn't that she cared about the candy. Lou Emma rescued the ribbon bow from the smashed box. That was enough. She had won *First Prize*.

"Now, remove your masks and let us see who you really are," Mrs. Biddle said. Off came the masks. There were no real surprises except one pillow-case ghost was a boy who belonged to the Baptist Sunday School.

"Each boy take a pumpkin half and match it with the girl who has the other half and we'll have refreshments." Mrs. Biddle looked wearily at the clock.

"Hey there!" The fat clown shouted at Lou Emma. Without his mask he was buck-toothed and bumptious. Their orange paper pumpkin halves matched exactly. "Aw right, Queenie, it's me'n you for the eats."

She tried to be polite and smile, but it was hard. Her crown kept falling off and her wand was in her way. "Wait'll I put these down," she said. Remembering the side porch she ran out there and put the

crown and wand on the railing. *That awful clown!*
But she must be nice to him.

The October night was chilly on her bare shoulders and she ran back into the warm room. The
clown was gone and Tommy was there, holding the
pumpkin half that matched her own.

"What happened?" she asked, pleased but puzzled,
too.

"Traded up," Tommy said briefly. "Le's go get
some cake."

At ten o'clock the party was over. After much
argument the Millers and Wackers had been given
permission to walk home. To be out at that hour on
Hallowe'en was exciting and vaguely dangerous. Every dark shadow brought squeals and shudders from
the girls. Only Hackberry strode boldly ahead. Barely
a block from the Biddles' Lou Emma remembered
her crown and wand on the side porch.

"You can go get'em tomorrow," Vinnie said, looking over her shoulder.

"No, they might blow away. Walk slow, and I'll
hurry."

Lou Emma ran back up Eclectic Avenue. She
could see Mrs. Biddle and Hilda moving around inside the house, cleaning up. She ran around to the
side porch, not wanting to disturb them, and sure she

could reach the porch railing. There, huddled against the shrubbery, crying as if her heart were broken, was Adelaide Moss.

"Oh, please," Lou Emma said. *"Please don't.* I didn't mean to get First Prize. Honest, I'm sorry." She reached toward Adelaide who jumped back as if she had been bitten.

"I could've won First Prize if I'd gone out half-nekkid the way you did. My mother wouldn't't've *let* me out of the house in a get-up with no sleeves, only straps."

"But . . . Miss Kate . . ." Lou Emma stammered before the violent attack.

"Hmph! You think Miss Kate Turner's going to marry your father? Well, I can tell you different. Nobody in this world wants a second-hand family, 'specially with you'n' that hateful Maddy Miller in it. Second-hand!"

She was gone, running faster than seemed possible in the Martha Washington costume. Lou Emma stood motionless. Adelaide's words repeated themselves. *Second-hand family . . . second-hand, second-hand, second-hand . . .*

On the porch above her Mrs. Biddle stepped out to shake a small rug. "Every year I say I'll never do this again, Hilda, and this time I mean it. That Moss child . . . honestly . . ." The door closed.

Slowly, Lou Emma joined the others.

"You could've gone to Topeka an' back," Vinnie complained.

"Where's your crown and wand?" Maddy asked.

Lou Emma put her hand to her head as if to locate the lost crown. "I couldn't find'em," she said, not even bothering to cross her fingers.

"What was wrong with Adelaide?" Eppie said. "She came tearing by here like the witches were after her. What happened?"

"I don't know," Lou Emma said dully.

"Get goin'," Hackberry ordered, "or Mama'll have the Law out."

They hurried through streets where Hallowe'en mischief had already been worked. Chicken coops in the sidewalk, front gates gone, a buggy on the steps of the Congregational Church. A flock of turkeys had been let out of Terry's Produce.

Maddy gave a little shriek. "Swish! I forgot to lock up Swish!"

They ran for home, pell-mell. Mrs. Wacker marched her three into the house, scolding them over their lateness. Maddy raced to the barn but Lou Emma walked in at the side door of the small brown house. She felt numb, as if nothing that mattered could ever happen to her again.

Then she saw her father, head down on the kitchen

table, a glass disk broken into two parts by his head.

"I'll shoot myself if it breaks," he had said, and *it was broken.*

She cried out and ran to him, and even when he jumped up and caught her in his arms she could not stop crying.

Maddy rushed in to say that Swish was fine as frog hair, and stopped open-mouthed. "Whatever in the world is the matter with Lou Emma?"

It took a long time, but at last as her father stroked her hair and Maddy brought wet wash cloths for her eyes, Lou Emma found her voice.

"You said you'd shoot yourself if the glass blank broke, Papa. And there it is . . . and your head was down . . . and I'm . . . I'm . . ."

"My poor tired little girl," Professor Miller said. "The glass blank didn't break at all. That's one of the extra disks. Garrett dropped it, but it doesn't matter now. The glass blank is now the *main mirror.*" He held up the six-inch mirror for her to see, its concave surface smooth and perfect. Lou Emma could see the oddly curved reflection of her teary face and tangled curls.

"It worked the way the book said it would," Maddy said, with awe.

"But suppose it had broken?" Professor Miller said. "I wouldn't shoot myself. Not as long as you two want me around. I got sleepy and I guess I dozed off."

"Why didn't you go on to bed?" Maddy said.

"Why'd you wait up if you were sleepy?" Lou Emma wondered.

"Maybe it's because I always liked to see pretty girls," their father said, and gave each one a gentle spank as he started them up the stairs.

Lou Emma waked with her curls tangled around her neck. In the darkness of the room she could barely make out her father sitting on the foot of the bed. He was looking over toward the Wacker house where a late lamp burned for Mr. Wacker.

"Papa," she whispered.

"Yes, Lou Emma, what is it?" He patted her groping hand.

She wanted to ask if it was really true that nobody in the world wanted a second-hand family. But at the last second she couldn't. It was too painful to hear it out loud again.

"Papa, the fortune teller at the party . . . I think it was Miss Lawrence . . . said that a dark woman was coming into my life."

She felt the little pressure of his hand that meant he had heard her.

"That sounds very nice," he said. "I certainly hope she's right."

Then he tucked the covers around Lou Emma's shoulders, picked up the pillow from the floor where Maddy had pushed it, and went away. Lou Emma heard him whistling softly as he walked down the stairs.

Chapter 18

Now the telescope was finished. It stood in the corner
of the front room. The heavy wooden brass-bound
tube was nearly six feet long. On the top was a jaunty
"dust cap" in green and gold that Miss Kate had made
to protect the mirror. Dr. Otto journeyed over from
Lawrence for the last figuring on the main mirror
and pronounced it a good job. Twice during the evening he bought Starlight Cocoa, and Lou Emma delighted in telling her father he hadn't seemed to think
it unscientific at all.

On the last night her profits amounted to $14.65
and Mr. Garrett insisted on paying extra for his cup
so the money for the eyepiece would be even-Steven.
She was proud to give the exact amount to Dr. Biddle.

Mr. Wacker had been in charge of making a stand to hold the telescope. It was constructed of some heavy lumber that he said the Santa Fe wasn't making any use of right now, and located a little north of Rehearsal Hall on the highest point of land on the campus. Leather straps were around the tube to hold it steady, for the least tremor could make the difference of a million miles.

The fifteenth of November was the night Professor Miller had chosen for the public showing of the telescope. At Dr. Biddle's urging, and because of the wide interest, the whole town was invited to come and view the full moon.

On the afternoon of the fourteenth Lou Emma walked home from school by way of Assembly Avenue to enjoy the posters in the store windows inviting the public to the Moon Gazing party. Miss Kate's Chapeaux featured a gray chiffon toque with a silver crescent moon holding the veil. She went into the shop.

"I've already sold three hats like that one," Miss Kate pointed to the toque in the window. "If that's commercializing the moon, let Mrs. Moss complain."

"Mrs. Moss paid a dressmaker to make Adelaide's Hallowe'en costume."

"Hmph. I'd hate to admit I had no more gumption than that."

"I never thought of that," Lou Emma said. For a

moment she felt a little triumph. Then she remembered Adelaide's words. *Second-hand family.*

Miss Kate looked at her sharply. "Something on your mind, Lou Emma?"

"No ma'am," Lou Emma answered slowly. "I was just wondering what to wear to the Moon Gazing party."

"Something warm," Miss Kate said. "Last night was below freezing."

Saturday, the fifteenth of November, was cold and clear. It was of the utmost importance to the Moon Gazing party that no clouds mar their view. All morning long Lou Emma and Maddy tracked in and out of the house, watching the sky.

"You can't hold back clouds by looking," Professor Miller said when he came in at noon for dinner. "Forget them. Write a poem. Read a book."

But between the pork chops and the tapioca, he, too, went out to look. After the dishes were dried, he walked over to Wackers' and came back with a frown on his face.

"Kate can't come to the Moon Gazing party until late. Can't . . . or won't. She has a special order for a wedding party at Waycross that has to be finished. Ridiculous!"

"In business you take orders when you get them,

and deliver the goods when you promise," Lou Emma said. Her father blinked, astonished.

"Where did you hear that, young lady?"

"Miss Kate. I wanted to go to the Tacky Party at Ellises' and not make Starlight Cocoa, and she said regular customers deserve regular service."

"Preposterous!" Professor Miller tossed a tea towel toward the sink. "Or—is it? I suppose in a crazy way, Kate's right."

"But the telescope was her idea," Maddy said. "She ought to be at the party. Can't you make an announcement that she thought of it, Papa?"

He shook his head. "Kate said if I so much as mentioned her name she'd get on her knees and pray for rain. But she'll try to come late."

The sun went down red. The wind went down with the sun. The temperature went down, down, down.

Wearing coats, sweaters, long underwear, heavy overshoes, caps, and muffled to the eyes in scarves the Millers and the Wackers piled into the Great Smith. The telescope tube had the place of honor next to the driver, and Mr. Wacker sat beside it to hold it steady.

"Going to drive your auto all winter?" Mr. Wacker asked.

"Oh no. Another week and I'll take off the wheels and put it up on blocks until Spring."

"I hear Hardy Garrett's already got his Stanley Steamer tucked into the barn alongside his pa's best cows," Mr. Wacker said.

"If it wasn't for Papa an' the Great Smith old Hardy'd still be in a mudhole in the middle of the road," Maddy said. "Him and his Stanley Steamer!"

"Watch your conversation *and* your grammar, Maddy," her father said.

"I like Mr. Garrett," Lou Emma said from the bottom layer of the back seat.

"Hardy's asked to take Miss Kate out when it snows," Vinnie said. "He's got this little sleigh shaped like a swan, with bells on the harness. He sparked Vona Ellis last winter and he'd drive her past our house after eleven o'clock and I'd hear the bells. Lots and lots of times."

"Vinnie, you never stayed awake till eleven in your life," her mother said.

Lou Emma thought, *I don't know why Vinnie is my best friend. She makes me madder'n anybody.*

"Look at that crowd!" Maddy gasped as they turned the corner.

Lou Emma struggled up from the bottom layer. There must have been a hundred people gathered around the telescope stand in the cold bright moonlight. More were coming, walking briskly, beating their arms against their chests, calling greetings to each other. It was a bigger crowd than had come out to watch the football game between the EKCC Buffaloes and the Grandview Teachers.

On the other side of Old Main some college boys had built a bonfire. The crowd moved back and forth, chilled by the night, warmed by the fire, their shadows wavering in the leaning flames.

Willing hands helped Professor Miller and Mr. Wacker lift the telescope tube from the Great Smith to the stand. The leather straps were buckled, the adjustment of the eyepiece began.

The light travels from the moon into the tube to the main mirror and back up the tube and . . . and . . . but where does it go THEN?

Chill that was panic, not weather, shook Lou Emma.

S'pose it doesn't work?

"Stand back please," she heard her father asking the eager crowd. "Just a moment now. Stand back . . . please . . ."

Instead of obeying she moved closer to him. If anything went wrong she ought to be near. Rule Number One.

Unable to endure not knowing, she whispered, "Is it all right?"

"Just a moment . . . Just a mo . . ."

Make it all right. Make it all right. Her fists were clenched in her mittens.

"There," she heard him say and the relief in his voice unclenched her fists. "It's all right now. And there's not a better eyepiece between here and Ursa Major, thanks to you."

"About ready, Professor?" Dr. Biddle asked respectfully.

"All ready," Professor Miller said and gave Lou Emma's mitten a squeeze.

Dr. Biddle cleared his throat. "Faculty members, students, friends of Eastern Kansas Classical College . . ."

The crowd stood patiently. Making a speech was part of the president's job; listening was part of their job. This time his "few words" were really few, and he called on the Congregational minister, who asked that God bless the instrument to His service and open the eyes of the people to His wonders.

Then Professor Miller talked a little about what they might see through the telescope tonight. The moon, the earth's nearest celestial neighbor, 238,257 miles away. The great craters on the moon, named for the early astronomers . . . Clavius, Tycho, Copernicus. And the flat plains, mistaken first for seas and still given the Latin name, *Marias.*

"Sea of Tranquillity, Sea of Clouds, Sea of Nectar," Lou Emma whispered, recalling the talk of the students around the Millers' kitchen table.

Then Professor Miller asked the crowd to form a line to look through the telescope, and suddenly Mr. Garrett took Lou Emma by the arm and placed her at the front of the line.

"This young lady had the git-up-and-git to buy the eyepiece," he boomed. "She deserves first look."

Amazingly it was there. *The moon was there.* Half-heard, half-understood things that her father told her came rushing back. They were all true.

In the sky the moon looked silvery, smooth, newly-made. In the eyepiece of the telescope it looked old . . . old as Time. Pockmarked, wrinkled, furrowed, but somehow beautiful beyond anything she had ever seen. The ancient mountains, the mysterious *Marias* . . .

Her father had to touch her arm and whisper, "Let the others come now. We can always come again."

That's right! We can always come again. Papa made the telescope, not by himself, that would have been selfish, but letting everybody help. Even me.

The long line waiting stretched far beyond the shadows of Old Main. People laughed, talked, shivered, and inched forward. But when they reached the telescope and looked into the eyepiece, like Lou Emma, they fell silent.

Tommy and his gang, with Hackberry tagging along, pushed, shoved, and wrestled in the long line. At the telescope they became quiet. Only J.T. coughed and choked, swallowing his chewing gum in surprise at the sight of the moon.

"The Heavens declare the Glory of God," the Methodist minister said solemnly after he had looked, and the reporter for the *Silver Bugle* put it in his notebook.

"Land o' hope an' glory!" Mrs. Wacker said and held up Joy to look.

Maddy came over to Lou Emma. "Don't look now, but Adelaide's next in line."

Lou Emma walked over to the bonfire to warm her feet. *I won't think about what Adelaide said.* Lou Emma put her mittened hands over her ears. *But where's Miss Kate? And where's . . . Hardy?*

"Get your hands off your ears," Maddy screamed. "We've all been looking for you. Papa'll be here for a while yet and Dr. Biddle's going to drive us home."

At the small brown house, they stood politely, feet freezing, while Dr. Biddle once more thanked Lou Emma for the eyepiece and told them what a fine man their father was.

"As if we didn't know," Maddy muttered as the surrey drove away.

Lou Emma caught her arm. "Did we leave the lamp burning?"

"Collywobbles, I don't remember. I don't think so."

They stared at the window where the green-shaded lamp was shining. "Who's in there?" Maddy said.

"It's two people," Lou Emma said. "We'd better go see."

Shoulder to shoulder, half-brave, half-scared, they came to the door. With enormous relief Lou Emma recognized Miss Kate. But the other person? Oh, *no!*

Hand holding tightly to hand, the Miller girls stepped inside.

"H-hello, Aunt Jesse," Lou Emma said.

"H-hello, Aunt Jesse," Maddy said.

Small, dainty, perfectly dressed for traveling, every gray hair in place, gold-framed eyeglasses gleaming, Miss Jesse Miller rose from the sofa and gave her nieces a peck on the cheek.

"When did you get here?" Maddy gulped.

"I arrived on the nine-twenty-seven Santa Fe. I wrote Cyrus weeks ago I was coming. There was no one at the depot, so I took a hack. A hired hack to my own brother's house!"

It seemed to Lou Emma that her aunt was reciting a list of sins. Her own sins, and Maddy's and their father's. And maybe Miss Kate's, too. *Why didn't we tell Papa about the letter? Why, oh, why?*

"I'm sure if Professor Miller had known . . ." Miss Kate said.

Miss Miller raised her eyebrows. "If Cyrus did not wish me to come, he had only to say so. I do not wish to be where I am not wanted."

"Oh Papa wanted you to come," Lou Emma plunged desperately. "Only he hasn't had much time lately. The telescope . . ."

"He hasn't made us clean up the house for more'n a month," Maddy said.

"I can see that," Miss Miller looked around the room.

All at once Lou Emma saw the room through her aunt's eyes. The barrel where the glass blank had been ground out into the main mirror was still in the middle of the floor. The spots of jeweler's rouge still speckled the sofa. The table was shoved crooked, piled with books. The window shades were at the top of the frame. One of Mr. Garrett's half-smoked cigars rested in a hand-painted dish.

"I told Cyrus all along that you girls could not manage alone."

"Most of the time they've done very well," Miss Kate said. "Recently . . ."

"This foolishness about a telescope," Miss Miller said. "Why, Cyrus can't lay carpet without losing half the tacks. Who got him into this?"

"Miss Kate," Maddy said, before Lou Emma could frame an answer. "The telescope was her idea first. And now she's got Papa into the notion of writing that textbook he's been talking about for forty-'leven years. Miss Kate can get him to do just about anything."

"How interesting, how very interesting," Miss Miller said.

It was a hateful grownup thing to say that didn't mean what its words said at all.

"Now girls," Miss Miller went on, "we must not keep Miss Turner any longer. It's getting late. For-

tunately, she was here in the kitchen when I arrived.
I was astonished to find . . . but then young women
are so independent these days."

Lou Emma noticed that her aunt said "young
women" not "young ladies."

"I was making up some cocoa to put on the back
of the stove," Miss Kate explained. "I knew they'd
be half-frozen, and . . ."

"Very kind," Miss Miller purred. "And since you
live next door . . . With the Wacker family? College
people, I presume."

"Not exactly," Miss Kate said. "But very good
friends."

"And you attended Eastern Kansas Classical College, Miss Turner?"

"No. My home is in Highbank." Miss Kate hesi-
tated, then she said, steadily, "I didn't go to college.
In fact, I only went to the second year in high school.
I went to work then. I'm a milliner."

"How interesting," Miss Miller repeated. "I am
sure that we are all grateful to you for your kindness
to Louisa Emmaline and Madeline Margaret."

*It's all going wrong, terribly wrong. And it's our
fault because we didn't tell Papa about the letter.
Why, oh why . . .* but Maddy was talking.

"Miss Kate saved Swish. She got Papa to let us
keep him."

"Swish is our goat," Lou Emma said, helplessly, as if she were forced to say it. "He's the one I kept the cigarettes for."

"If you will excuse me . . ." Miss Miller took from her handbag the familiar cut-glass vial of smelling salts and held it to her nose. "This has been a long, trying trip. To find goats, cigarettes, barrels in the front room of my brother's home. *And no one to meet me at the depot . . .*"

At that moment the Great Smith turned in at the yard. Professor Miller came into the unhappy silence that followed his sister's last remark.

"Hello, girls. Kate, we missed you. It was a big success, and all your idea, even if you wouldn't . . . let . . . me . . . say . . . so." His words rolled out one by one as he saw his sister. "Jesse? Where did you come from?"

"The question, Cyrus, is where have you been?" Miss Miller presented her cheek and her brother dutifully kissed it.

"Up at the college. My astronomy classes . . . but I forgot, I haven't written you about that. I meant to, of course, but time gets away. Why didn't you tell me you were coming?"

"I wrote to you weeks ago," Miss Miller said. "You didn't reply, but you have always been a poor correspondent. It never occurred to me that your only sister might not be welcome. But I suppose you have your reasons."

She means Miss Kate! Lou Emma cringed at her aunt's icy tones.

"Stop it, Jesse. I didn't get any letter."

Now they could no longer go on hiding what they had done. Lou Emma knew it, and she realized Maddy did, too, for she heard her sister take a deep breath.

"You didn't get the letter because I threw it in the river."

"I did it too," Lou Emma said. "I put it back in Maddy's pocket without her knowing. It was because of Adelaide and the nose-bleed, and no matter what Mrs. Moss says, Adelaide asked for it. And The Creepers were coming . . ."

As she spoke she knew she was telling grownups a secret thing and now The Creepers would never return. But it had to be done.

"The river? You threw my letter into the river?" Out came the smelling salts. The sharp, acrid scent reached Lou Emma's nose.

"Please, Jesse," Professor Miller said. "It sounds terrible, but the girls usually have some reason for what they do. *The Creepers?* Now let's get this whole thing straightened out."

"There are some things no one can straighten out,"

Miss Miller said tragically. "Cyrus, what have you done to these poor little motherless girls?"

"Oh, come now, Jesse, the girls and I are getting along fine. There may be a few things out of place, but . . ." He looked around the room. "Kate? Where's Kate gone?"

They all looked then, and Lou Emma realized she should have known when she felt the chill wind around her ankles that Miss Kate had opened the front door and gone quietly away.

"She's gone home, I guess. Her coat's gone, too."

"Perhaps that's better," Miss Miller said. "I can hardly tell you, Cyrus, how amazed I was."

"Kate's gone?" Professor Miller repeated. "Why did she go?"

"It's very late," Miss Miller said. "An unmarried female . . ."

"Nonsense! I'm going after her."

"Cyrus, I beg you . . ."

The door slammed, cutting off Miss Miller's words.

"I'm sorry about the letter, Aunt Jesse," Lou Emma said. "Neither one of us meant for it to go in the river. It just happened. We acted awful."

"That dog was chasing us," Maddy said. "We should've told Papa right away, only we didn't. We *could* say it was Rule Number Two, but it wouldn't be true."

"My poor little motherless nieces," Miss Miller touched her blue eyes with a lacy handkerchief. "My heart aches for you. You can go back to Cleveland with me."

As Lou Emma and Maddy stared, open-mouthed, at each other, Professor Miller burst into the room, white-faced and wild-eyed.

"She's gone! Kate's gone. She's not at Wackers'. They don't know where she is. Hepzie and the buggy are in the stable. The temperature's three below zero. Where could she be?" He grabbed Lou Emma. "Did she say anything to you?"

"No, Papa. Not even 'good night.' "

"To you, Maddy? Think! Think!"

"I am thinking, Papa. Miss Kate didn't say anything, really, except when Aunt Jesse asked her if she went to EKCC, and she said she'd only been as far as the second year of high school, and . . ."

"Jesse, is this true?"

Miss Miller looked frightened. "Yes, but surely a simple question . . ."

"It was not a simple question, and you know it."

"But Cyrus, an uneducated young woman . . . a milliner . . ."

"Miss Kate has her own business," Lou Emma said bravely.

"And the best catch in town waiting to take her out when it snows," Maddy said.

"Hardy Garrett! She's gone out with Hardy," Professor Miller struck his palm with his fist. "I should have left him in that mudhole."

"No, Papa," Lou Emma shook his arm. "She wouldn't go out with Hardy without a hat. There's her new hat on the table."

A modish brown velvet with a crimson band rested on H-O-G.

"I hope you're right." Professor Miller stroked the brown velvet. "I've got to find Kate. There is something I have to tell her."

Lou Emma's heart gave a little lurch and beat faster, harder.

"It can surely wait until morning," Miss Miller said.

"It *cannot*," he shouted. "It cannot wait any more time *at all*. Come along, girls, we're going to find Kate."

"You're not going to drag your poor little . . ."

"Jesse, if you call these girls my poor little motherless daughters one more time I will not be responsible for what I do."

In spite of themselves, Lou Emma and Maddy giggled.

"Really, Cyrus!" Miss Miller took out her cut-glass

vial of smelling salts and sniffed it twice. "I have never been spoken to in such a tone . . ."

"Then it's time you were," Professor Miller said. "And another thing—you've ruled me with this confounded cut-glass battle-axe long enough."

He strode over, took the vial from his sister, opened the door and threw it as far as he could into the icy night.

"Ready, girls?"

"Yessir."

"Wait, please wait." It was a different tone from any Lou Emma ever heard from her aunt before. "I didn't mean . . . believe me, Cyrus, I only wanted . . ."

Suddenly Professor Miller smiled. "All right, Jesse. Sit down and take it easy. You've had quite an evening. When we get back I'm sure you'll be feeling better."

"Yes, Cyrus," she said meekly, "I'm sure I will and—good luck."

Fortunately, the Great Smith had not had time to become completely cold. The engine started with the first twist of the crank. They rolled out to the street. "I have no idea which way to go," Professor Miller said.

"Maybe she wanted to look through the telescope

after all," Maddy suggested. "Maybe she went up to the college."

"It hardly seems likely, but . . ." Professor Miller turned the wheel toward the campus. They spun over the iron-hard streets.

The campus was deserted. In the cold glitter of the moon, not one person was to be seen. They circled Old Main twice.

"It's not like Kate to be foolish," Professor Miller said. "Nothing on her head, the temperature below zero and dropping fast."

"Berkemyer's sells hot chocolate," Maddy said. "They keep open late."

But just as they reached Assembly Avenue the street lights went out.

"Eleven o'clock," Lou Emma said.

One lone wagon was at the hitching-rack, the team huddled under horse blankets. No lights showed in the store fronts. They drove slowly the length of the street and back again. Berkemyer's was as empty of life as the mountains of the moon.

"She's got to be somewhere," Professor Miller hammered on the steering wheel with his fur-lined gauntlets. "She couldn't disappear into thin air."

"Papa," Lou Emma said hesitantly, "sometimes when I miss all my arithmetic problems and the Music Teacher catches me not singing I go in the kitchen when I get home and cook stuff. Easy stuff, like gingerbread. Do you s'pose Miss Kate could've gone back to the millinery shop?"

"Making hats at eleven o'clock?" Maddy said scornfully. "Silly."

"It's not silly at all," Professor Miller said. "When my classes go badly I translate Greek poetry. Easy stuff. But we've looked in the window. There's no sign of anyone at Miss Kate's Chapeaux."

"Behind the curtain," Lou Emma said. "That's where she'd be. There's a back door on the alley and a Coleman gasoline lamp in case the electricity fails."

But even as she was talking her father turned the Great Smith into the alley, and next door to the *Silver Bugle,* a window showed a gleam of light.

The hand-brake crunched, and Professor Miller was over the side of the Great Smith, the girls scrambling after him. He jerked the back door open and showed a startled Kate Turner, stitching on a white bridal veil. Her eyes were red, her nose was pink.

"Kate! You've been crying!" he said.

"I have not," Miss Kate said fiercely. "What are you three doing out this time of night?"

"Looking for you," Lou Emma said. "Papa's got something to tell you."

"Papa thought you were out with Hardy," Maddy

said. "And he wisht he'd left him in that mudhole."

Lou Emma was almost sure she saw Miss Kate's lip twitch as if she were trying not to smile. She snipped a thread and held up the bridal veil.

"Hardy's taking me to Waycross to deliver this tomorrow."

"Oh no he's not," Professor Miller said firmly. "I'm taking you to Waycross or wherever you want to go. From this time forward."

Miss Kate dropped the bridal veil. "And who gave you permission?"

"Nobody—yet. But you will, won't you? Dear, darling, managing, independent Kate? Tonight at the Moon Gazing party the whole thing fell apart for me because you weren't there. I didn't care if nobody in Gloriosa saw the moon if you weren't there to see it. That's what I came to tell you." He stopped, stripped off his fur-lined gauntlets and took Miss Kate's hands. "I love you, Kate. Will you marry me?"

He pulled her into his arms and only quick work by Lou Emma kept the bridal veil from being trampled.

"But how about the girls?" Miss Kate said. "Lou Emma? Maddy? Do you want me, too?"

"Rule Number One," the Miller girls shouted as if they had practiced it for weeks. "The Family Sticks Together, No Matter What."

"I'm the luckiest woman in the world," Miss Kate said, an arm around each of them. "A ready-made family."

A wave of pure happiness came over Lou Emma, and she breathed deep the scent of rose cologne. A ready-made family. A second-hand family. What a lot of difference there was in the words. *Why'd I ever listen to Adelaide, anyway?*

"But I'm afraid your sister, Jesse, isn't going to be pleased," Miss Kate said with a little frown pulling her eyebrows together. "I'm sorry."

"Don't worry about Jesse. She's at home right now making plans to welcome you to the family. I'll guarantee it," Professor Miller said.

"You should've been there when Papa threw out her smelling-salts," Maddy said, her eyes dancing.

"But Aunt Jesse means well," Lou Emma said anxiously, then laughed at herself. She was too happy to worry about anything tonight.

"All right, girls, out to the Great Smith," Professor Miller said.

"Papa, it's below zero!"

"Papa, we'll freeze solid!"

"*SANGUINE SATURNINI!*" He shouted, but he was laughing, too. They scooted out the door.

In the back seat, muffled to their nosetips in a heavy laprobe, the Miller girls waited.

"We're not going back to Cleveland with Aunt Jesse. We're going to have a mother of our very own," Lou Emma gloated.

"Shoot, Papa'd never have let us go," Maddy said, then she added, "Stepmother."

"What you call anybody doesn't matter," Lou Emma said, and suddenly realized this was true. "She'll belong to us; we'll belong to her."

"It's going to be a lot different," Maddy said.

"Different can be nice," Lou Emma said, snuggling deeper in the laprobe.

"Tomorrow let's ask Papa what that means. You know, what he says?"

"Uh-uh," Lou Emma said. "Uh-*uh*. Let's ask Miss Kate to ask him."

ABOUT THE AUTHOR

Alberta Wilson Constant was born in Texas but spent much of her life in Oklahoma. While attending Oklahoma City University she was encouraged by several of her professors to write. Later, she took classes in professional writing at the University of Oklahoma. The Oklahoma country, with its short, exciting span of statehood and its colorful people, has been the inspiration of several of her books.

Mrs. Constant lives in Independence, Missouri, with her husband and two children.

ABOUT THE ARTISTS

As a successful husband-and-wife team, Beth and Joe Krush have illustrated well over fifty books for children. Both Mr. and Mrs. Krush attended the Philadelphia Museum of Art. Each of them now teaches illustration: Joe Krush at the Museum's school, The Philadelphia College of Art, and Beth Krush at Moore College of Art. Mr. Krush is chairman of the Illustration Committee of the Philadelphia Art Alliance.

The Krushes and their son live in Wayne, Pennsylvania.